hide and
SEEK

Stories about
being young and gay/lesbian

Also by Jenny Pausacker

What Are Ya?
Mr Enigmatic
Getting Somewhere

hide and SEEK

Stories about being young and gay/lesbian

edited by Jenny Pausacker

MANDARIN

Published 1996 under the Mandarin imprint
by Reed for Kids
17–23 Redwood Drive, Dingley, Vic. 3172
a division of Reed International Books Australia Pty Ltd

Typeset in Goudy by Abb-typesetting
Printed and bound in Australia by Australian Print Group

National Library of Australia
cataloguing-in-publication data:

Hide and seek: stories about being young and gay/lesbian.

ISBN 1 86330 752 4.

1. Short stories, Australian. 2. Lesbians - Australia- Fiction. 3. Gays -
Australia - Fiction. 4. Lesbians' writings, Australian. 5. Gays' writings,
Australian.
Pausacker, Jenny.

A823.0108353

The author and publisher gratefully acknowledge BlackWattle Press for
permission to reproduce Dean Kiley's 'staying in'.

Thanks to everyone who helped with this anthology, especially Agnes Nieuwenhuizen who suggested the idea, Maryann Ballantyne who developed it, Gary Dunne who provided invaluable help and information and Mark Macleod for stimulating and entertaining discussions throughout.

Contents

Introduction

The main purpose of this introduction is to give me a chance to confess that the subtitle of the anthology— 'stories about being young and gay/lesbian'—is a bit misleading. Yes, there are stories about being young and gay or lesbian here. However, there are also stories about being young and confused, curious, undecided, attracted to both sexes or wondering how to react to people who are (or may be) gay ... but try fitting all of that into a subtitle.

The range of subject matter is matched by a range of styles. Some writers have taken a realist approach, some experiment with style and form and others give a new twist to established genres—a gay ghost story, for example, and a girls' own adventure story. You'll come across a monologue complete with stage directions, a high school reunion speech, a story in verse, a story in letters, stories told mainly through dialogue, colloquial stories and stories whose narrative style is carefully and intricately wrought.

The contributors themselves are as varied as their stories—writers best known for their adult fiction or non-fiction; writers for young adults; writers who have mainly written for the gay press; established writers and writers who are just starting out. I wasn't concerned with the sexual preference of the contributors: although I know some people believe that lesbian and gay themes should only be dealt with by lesbian and gay writers, my own particular form of idealism consists of a desire to see gay men and lesbians appearing in fiction as often as in life. So my main criterion, when I was drawing up the guest list for this anthology, was that the contributors had already written about gay experience at some point, as an indication that they had thought about the basic issues and were ready to tackle some of the more complex aspects of the theme.

Despite all this range and variety, the stories are linked closely together by their common concern with being young—somewhere between the early teens and twenties—and being gay. It's an important nexus. True, we live in a society where the laws relating to homosexuality have (on the whole) been liberalised, where there are lesbian and gay characters in sitcoms and articles about gay issues in glossy magazines. But the difficulties associated with being *young* and gay haven't changed much. We worry about youth homelessness without recognising that, of the 20,000 plus young Australians estimated to be homeless, about one in four is gay.[1] We worry about the rate of youth suicide but newspaper reports never include the fact that 'Gay and lesbian youth are two or three times more likely to attempt suicide than other young people'.[2] Clearly, there is an urgent need for accurate and affirming descriptions of young lesbian and gay experience.

Mind you, there are books and stories like this around, as long as you know where to find them. Try Mark Macleod's anthology *Ready or Not*, for starters.

Witi Ihimaera's short story 'Who Are You Taking to the School Dance, Darling?' (in *Crossing*), Fiona Kidman's 'Nobody Else' (*Just Seventeen*), Peter McFarlane's 'Coober' (*Lovebird*) and Nadia Wheatley's 'The Most Unforgettable Character I Have Ever Met' (*The Night Tolkien Died*) would all have fitted comfortably into this collection. Elizabeth Riley's *All That False Instruction*, my own *What Are Ya?*, Kate Walker's *Peter* and William Taylor's *The Blue Lawn* are examples of adult or young adult novels from Australia and New Zealand that deal with young men and women who are questioning their sexuality—and now there's a whole new generation of writers like Graeme Aitken, Paula Boock, Fiona McGregor, Gina Schien and Christos Tsiolkas. And Laurel Clyde and Marjorie Lobban's impressive booklist *Out of the Closet and Into the Classroom* surveys over 120 books from Australia and overseas with main or peripheral young gay characters.

My main aim in editing *Hide and Seek* has been to cross as many boundaries as possible—boundaries dividing people on the basis of sexual preference, the boundary between adult and young adult fiction, the boundary that has separated gay writing from a general readership. I hope this anthology will remind adult readers of all the questions they asked themselves when they were growing up, just as I hope that the stories will reach out both to young adults who are wondering whether they might be gay and to the friends and schoolmates, teachers and relatives who are in a position to make life either easier or far more difficult for them.

But most of all, I hope that everyone who picks up this book will enjoy, as much as I have, the honesty, the exploration and the sheer virtuosity of the writers in this collection.

Jenny Pausacker
September 1995

[1] As Long as I've Got My Doona: A Report on Lesbian and Gay Youth Homelessness, 1995. Available from 2010, PO Box 213, Glebe 2037.

[2] US Department of Health and Human Services, Task Force on Youth Suicide Report, 1989.

A True Kindness

Bron Nicholls

Obstruction. Impasse. Shut-down. When we get out of this, there will be one compensating factor: I will have a huge collection of words for STUCK. Imagine my eloquence. Your Honour, my client murdered her boyfriend during a fit of Spanner-in-the-Works. She suffers from Deadlock Phobia.

Keran squeezes her fist around an empty orange-juice carton. She has propped herself against the only tree in front of Gilbert's Garage—Windscreens Fitted, All Motor Repairs—in the small town of Beaufort, 160 kms from home. Time 12.00 noon; air temperature 40° in the shade; and out there, bare-headed under the sun, Malcolm and a mechanic are peering at the innards of Keran's mother's red Saab, which had a paroxysm of coughing and then stopped with a death rattle as Malcolm steered into the yard. Valves, circulation, combustion chambers—it sounds like medical talk, so it's Malcolm's business, really. And Keran has a headache coming on like the start of a Grand Prix.

Across the glaring white gravel yard, the mechanic shuts the bonnet of the Saab. Malcolm heads for the small circle of shade under the tree. His face has turned pink, his T-shirt is patched with sweat. Keran pushes a carton of juice into his hand. 'How bad is it?' She's referring to the car.

'I'm okay.' He slumps to the ground, leans against the

tree. 'The motor's got a broken head gasket. Radiator ran dry. We overheated.'

'But Mummy said she filled everything!'

'Keran, we can now deduce that your mother meant the car was stocked with Minties, muesli bars, tissues and petrol. I doubt she's even aware that cars need water. Sorry! It's my fault, I was driving. But when you don't own a car you don't think of checking everything.'

'Cut the *mea culpa*. Just tell me how much and how long to fix. One hour? I've got a filthy headache, I need to find a washroom and a cooler place to wait.'

Malcolm opens the carton of warm orange juice; it drips onto his jeans as he gulps at the spout. Disgusted, Keran looks away, over the shimmering metal road and a sale-yard of farm machinery, to some bleak bare hills close to the town. 'I get it. Expensive and a long wait. Right. I wonder if air-conditioning has reached this out-post. You coming with me or are you going to play assistant surgeon to that long-haired mechanic?'

A slightly hysterical giggle escapes from Malcolm. 'Kerry, you're not going to believe this. It's a Back-to-Beaufort this weekend, starting tonight. All accommodation is booked out. We could wait for a late train to Ballarat but Jim has a better idea.'

Keran discovers she no longer cares about her white jeans. She seats herself on the ground, rubs her forehead with her knuckles. 'What are you trying to say, Malcolm?'

'You can't expect a small town to keep every part for every foreign car. Jim's phoning Melbourne now, the gasket will come tonight, he'll do the job tomorrow morning. It's the best anyone can do.'

'Where are the keys? Mum will have planted a ton of aspirin somewhere.'

'Listen, Jim is a good chap. He says we can stay at their place—he lives with a friend—the other side of those hills. It's a very kind offer.'

'And the car isn't the only thing with a cracked gasket. Mal, you can do what you like. I'm catching a taxi back to Ballarat—I don't care if it costs the earth.' Keran stands up, steadies herself against the tree, gazes upon Malcolm as if she has never seen him before. 'When you pick me up tomorrow, it might be best to go all the way back. The car's obviously unreliable. I don't want to get stuck halfway up some godforsaken mountains.'

She strides across the gravel, shouts at the boy attending the petrol pumps. 'Is there a washroom?'

The boy points to the far end of the garage. Jim comes out of the workshop, waves an oily red cloth, like a flag. 'No problems, Malcolm, it's on its way. Would you two like a cuppa and a sandwich?'

It's an old ute with a bench seat covered with a scrap of tartan blanket. The blanket has a doggy pong, only slightly diminished by the dust blowing through the open windows. Jim takes it easy on the corrugated dirt road but each bump feels like a hammer-blow in Keran's head. She leans against the door, bracing herself against the jolts.

Malcolm sits in the middle, hands between his knees, confused and apprehensive. Kerry having a whinge when plans go wrong, that's nothing new. But this cold, drawn-out hostility is uncustomary. Rudeness in the face of generosity is taboo in Malcolm's code. And Jim not being a chatty type, Malcolm can't imagine what he thinks of the situation. When Kerry returned to the garage after a futile quest for an available cab, Jim's only response was: 'I'm glad you've changed your mind. I think you'll like Innisfree.'

The name rings a vague bell for Malcolm. He can use it, anyway, to break this ice. 'Why did you call your place Innisfree? It's Irish, isn't it?'

'It's from a poem about a place in Ireland—'

'Ah yes! Yeats. "The Lake Isle of Innisfree". Thought I'd forgotten everything we did in high school.'

'Well, we just liked the sound of it.'

'Yes, it does sound sort of—um—free!'

My gawd, thinks Keran. Don't try so hard, Malcolm, you'll crack something else. And that reminds me ...

'Jim?' She turns to shout across Malcolm. 'Why didn't we know the Saab was overheating?' What she means is: Why didn't Mal look at the temperature gauge during the whole bloody trip?

Jim shouts back. 'The downside of perfect sealed-off air-conditioning. It doesn't let you smell something going wrong in the engine.'

Malcolm, occasionally, can read Kerry's mind. 'You wanted me to drive, Keran, despite the car being new to me. The dashboard was terrifying—I couldn't tell the clock from the CD player!'

Jim laughs. Malcolm begins to relax. Keran decides: Collusion is what men are best at. She returns her gaze to the stony hills and dry zigzag gullies, and rabbits also zigzagging, as if blind, before scuttling to hide underground.

The road is climbing, twisting. Kerry is wondering how much more she can stomach, when Jim slows and stops on the crest of a hill.

'There's our place. The blue roof. What do you reckon?'

The sky-blue tin roof is almost hidden behind trees. Like an embracing arm, the range curves around the northern end of a little valley; the solitary house is halfway down the nearest slope and at the bottom a creek flanked with willows and wattles meanders southward. Black-and-white cows are feeding on a broad ribbon of grass along the creek flat. Like everything Keran has encountered today, it seems unbelievable.

'Wow,' says Malcolm. 'It's beautiful. Did you build the house?'

'Heavens, no, it's about ninety years old! We bought it six years ago, fixed it up. A big move for Pat and me—we came from the city. The cows aren't ours, just the dogs. You like dogs?'

Too late now if we don't, thinks Keran, as a whitish fat Labrador and a big gangly Irish setter come hurtling up the track. The red dog leaps into the back of the ute. Jim gets out to help the fat one aboard. 'That's Gertrude, she's old. The crazy one is Oscar.'

The happiness in his voice makes Kerry smile, in spite of herself. For the first time she looks properly at Jim. Mmm. He's good looking—or he will be, when he's cleaned up. He and his Pat, whoever she is, they're lucky. It must be nice to have a life this simple. And all under your own control ...

From the back verandah, which faces east, you can watch the hills across the valley turn coppery pink in the low sunlight. The cows have gone home; magpies sing softly in the orchard below the house. The dogs are asleep under a long table which bears the remains of a generous meal—salads, cold meats, homemade pickles and fresh bread, cool white wine.

Malcolm stretches out in his easy chair. He is idling now but it hasn't been easy, waiting to see which way Keran would go. She has been polite and quiet, an unusual combination. Headache gone, she reckons. Must ask Patrick what he gave her. Something 'a bit stronger than aspirin', he said. It certainly worked fast.

There was only one tense moment during the customary brief exchange of personal histories by which strangers try to establish trust. Malcolm began with: 'We were on our way to the Grampians—a few days of sight-seeing before settling back at uni. Our second year. It's going to be med for me and law for Kerry.'

'Ah, "A Daniel come to judgement!"' Patrick nodded. 'Yes, I can see you at the bar.'

'A Danielle, don't you mean?' Keran smiled coldly. 'And on the bench, eventually.'

'Good for you.' Patrick's smile was contrite. 'Forgive me. Jim is too sweet to correct my Political Incorrectness and the dogs are too lazy.'

Fortunately, Keran laughed. Malcolm gulped down all his wine as if it was water. Probably why his thoughts are now a bit fuzzy. Can't recall what kind of text-books Pat said he edits. Perhaps he didn't say.

'So what attracts you to reconstructive surgery, Malcolm? Apart from the obvious.'

'The obvious? Oh, you mean the money! I suppose that's part of it. Doesn't everyone want to be well paid for their hard work?'

Patrick smiles patiently. 'I did say: apart from the obvious.'

'Right. Well, it's not because I see myself in a fancy clinic doing cosmetic jobs on people who think they deserve a more fashionable face or a smaller backside or whatever. And that's not a criticism of your father, Kerry, quite the opposite. The work he does on accident victims—restoring a person's face, or a hand—that's really something, in my opinion. That's what I'd like to do, ultimately. Does that answer your question?'

'It does indeed.' Patrick leans across the table, refills Malcolm's wine glass. Malcolm wonders: How old is he? He doesn't get much sun, hair wispy on top but not grey, all of him too thin. Eyes sharp as a bird. Nice mouth … But there's something I'm missing. Like not seeing the message on the temperature gauge.

'Have you always been a freelance editor, Patrick?'

'Heavens, no. Only since coming here. That's merely my contribution to the household fund.' With a bare foot he rubs Oscar's belly. Still asleep, the dog stretches out, sighs with contentment. Jim and Patrick laugh together, as if the dog has done something amazing.

Malcolm refuses to be distracted. 'So what else do you do?'

'Oh, reading for pleasure. Cooking likewise. We've managed to get fruit out of that old orchard. I've even learnt to prune Jim's rose garden.'

Keran seems to wake from a trance. 'The roses are beautiful. Especially the pale pinks. I adore roses.'

'I'll give you some cuttings,' says Jim.

'They'd never grow for me. I don't have a green thumb.'

Patrick laughs again. 'For roses, a pink thumb is probably best.'

Keran decides that Patrick really is a supercilious prick. She returns to the list she has been writing in her head: Things To Be Done before the new term starts.

Malcolm suspects himself of losing track of the conversation. He giggles. 'I think I've had too much wine.'

'You're okay,' says Patrick in a suddenly subdued tone. '"Receive what cheer you may. The night is long that never finds the day."'

'I'm going to make us a big pot of tea,' says Jim. As he moves behind the chairs, he touches the back of Pat's neck, an intimate touch, as if for three seconds there are no visitors. Malcolm quickly closes his eyes.

So that's why Keran winked at me, earlier. She knew straight off. So what? They're still nice people. But I bet we won't be telling Keran's mother who we stayed with!

He giggles again and feels for the edge of the table, to put his glass down. Patrick gently takes the almost-empty glass from Malcolm's hand. 'It's safe to open your eyes, Malcolm.'

Keran stands up. 'Is it okay if I have that shower you offered before dinner?'

'Of course. I've put towels in your room. Sun-dried sheets on the bed. You'll get the southerly breeze if you leave a window open.'

'Thank you for dinner and everything.' She gives Malcolm a pitiless glance, looks into the kitchen to say goodnight to Jim. 'I hope you're making that tea strong!'

The sun has been down for some time; the only light for the verandah comes through the kitchen windows and the screen door of the hall, yet Jim places cups and pours tea as if he always does this in the dark. Patrick says: 'We keep time with the birds here, so drink this, then we'll all turn in. The tea's not strong. Why spoil the benefits of a good wine?'

The tea has a scent of oranges. Malcolm drinks thirstily. He notices the pale half-moon high above the hills, which are now silver-grey. The birds have gone quiet; a couple of frogs murmur to each other, with long spaces between their brief exchanges. Malcolm isn't accustomed to so much peace. After about ten minutes, when Jim and Patrick quietly begin to clear the table, he hops in to help. He doesn't want to be left alone in the dark deep stillness.

Malcolm wakes suddenly. A giant is clomping over the roof, several giants, laughing, chattering, coughing. Malcolm waits for his heart to slow down; listens, during the lull from above, to Keran's uneven breathing. Beyond the open window the black sky is glittering with stars.

At the end of the hall a dim light glows near the bathroom. When Malcolm gets to the door, it opens. Patrick stares, blank faced, as if for a moment he has forgotten … 'Ah. It's you. Everything all right?'

'Yes. Just got woken by something on the roof.'

'Possums. At the half-moon they do Irish jigs.'

'I'm glad that's all it is!'

Patrick leaves the bathroom light on. As he walks past, Malcolm can't avoid turning to stare. Above the pyjama pants, Patrick's bare back is dotted with small dark smudges. Automatically, silently, Malcolm recites: Kaposi's sarcoma lesions. A malignant tumour arising from blood vessels in the skin. Rare except in patients with AIDS.

He closes the door behind him. Before dinner, Malcolm was amused at the charm of this room: timber walls painted pale pink and deep green, just like the roses from the garden for heavensake, and the towels all in a row, nothing out of place. He had been afraid to disturb anything. Now he is afraid for another reason. He tears off half a metre of toilet paper to lift the seat. Scrubs his hands in near-boiling water before having a piss and again after pressing the flush button. He knows this is ludicrous; he can't believe he is doing it. 'I'm a medical student!' he whispers aloud. 'I'm supposed to be rational.'

Outside the open window a possum cackles harshly, as if in mockery.

Dawn. A clear sky. Another hot day coming up.

Urgently in need of strong tea, Keran sneaks out to the kitchen. Jim is there, dressed for work, and stirring something in a huge basin. 'Morning. D'you want some porridge?'

'Not for me. Can I make a pot of tea?'

'Kettle's just boiled. Toast, fruit, it's all there.'

'Tea will do for now. That's an enormous lot of porridge.'

'It's for the dogs. A sort of muesli, really. They demand raisins and fresh chopped apples in it. Pat and I get the left-overs.'

Keran laughs and her forehead throbs like an echo. 'Where's the coolest place outside, Jim?'

'The front verandah until midday, then you keep moving slowly round the house. But feel free to stay inside. Pat's got his own study. I'll phone when I'm finished—five, six hours—then Pat will drive you into town.'

'What a bother for you both. I am sorry.'

'Don't be silly.' A whining duet begins at the back door. 'I'm going to let the dogs in now, so if you want some peace, try the dining room.'

Keran decides to stay here all morning. The light is filtered through a huge Douglas fir tree outside the window, there's a wide sofa against a wall of books, creamy white roses in the centre of a round table. She sinks into the sofa. Ah yesss ... I could sleep here. Mal's nightmares kept waking me. What's wrong with him? With us? It's like we fizzled out at the same time as the car. Not stuck, but unstuck

Kerry sleeps. She doesn't hear Jim's ute departing, nor Patrick peeping in and then gently reclosing the door.

'We've been together almost a year. Everyone expects us to get engaged when we're twenty-one. Now we're suddenly strangers—within twenty-four hours. There are too many differences between us, that's the trouble.'

Malcolm and Patrick have stopped to rest in some deep shade. The dogs are wallowing in the creek, snuffling among willow roots. 'They can smell water-rats. They never catch any but they keep hoping.' Patrick watches, while Malcolm talks.

'Her family has always had money. Anything they want—Kerry takes it for granted. She hates me telling people that my parents own a shoe factory, that they worked like peasants to send three kids to good schools. So I keep my mouth shut now.'

'And feel resentful at the same time?' Patrick throws a stick into the water. Both dogs scramble for it.

'A bit … yes.'

'So what are you going to do about it?'

'Nothing, I guess. I'm too scared Kerry will stop loving me.'

'Ah. But "Love is not love which alters when it alteration finds". You agree?'

'Is that another quote? You've got a peculiar way of speaking, Pat. No offence meant.' Malcolm swerves away as Oscar wheels to a halt, shakes his wet coat, offers Patrick one end of the stick for a game of Tug. Patrick's words follow the rhythm of the game.

'Small differences shouldn't—destroy love. They irritate. Or keep us—intrigued. But concealed similarities— threaten us. Things we—don't like in ourselves—mirrored back.' Oscar drops his end of the stick, Patrick chucks it to the opposite bank, the dogs hurl themselves across the narrow creek. 'And I'm not talking about the body.'

Malcolm is wishing he hadn't started this conversation. 'I can't see how that concerns Keran and me. You don't know us. You're not like us at all.'

Patrick grins. 'I don't agree. Rewind me twenty years and there I am, a typical uni student: ambitious, impatient, narrow minded, self-righteous. You look shocked, Malcolm. Why?' Malcolm's mouth has dropped open. 'Ah. You're thinking: And what's he got to show for twenty years? Not a lot, I'll admit. But the little I've got is due to love that "bears it out even to the edge of doom". And my peculiar way of speaking is a habit from my insecure youth, when I quoted Shakespeare to give me courage and make an impression. I'm not so very different to you. And maybe you and Keran are more alike than you've noticed.'

Malcolm struggles to control his voice, his anger. 'I don't wish to discuss this any further. I don't see how you can presume to give advice—about love—to other people, to—' the words spurt out, unstoppable, 'to normal people!'

Unruffled, Patrick replies: 'I do tend to be presumptuous. That's true.' He looks around for the dogs; they have found some shade and are steadily chewing at opposite ends of the same stick. He smiles.

Malcolm feels suddenly ill. Never has he spoken like that. Thoughts, yes. But never ever spoken. 'Patrick, I apologise. I didn't mean to offend you.'

'You haven't, Mal. Your opinions about me don't matter a scrap. I need my energy for more important things than taking offence. Let's go and make some lunch, any longer and it will be too hot on the hillside, for me. I'm not well. As you know.'

'Yes. That's why I'm apologising.'

'Thought so. Well, pity is something I can do without,

pity and condescension. You know, Malcolm, I liked you better when you were being an honest bigoted homophobe.' Patrick puts his hat on. 'Gertrude! Oscar! Home now.'

Every breath needed for the steep climb. The white grass reflects the sun like a mirror. Malcolm feels light-headed, probably from lack of breakfast. He recalls how he refused the great-looking omelette Pat offered; how he peeled an orange and lied about not being hungry.

The dogs are panting, keeping close to Patrick. On the flat under the orchard, Patrick has a brief coughing paroxysm. Malcolm gazes back down the hill. He feels useless and afraid. 'You're so isolated here! What happens when you need a doctor?'

'I am a doctor.'

Malcolm laughs. 'Why didn't I guess? Which field?'

'Physician. Specialising in the heart. Gave it up six years ago to come here with Jim. And to prolong my own life.'

Malcolm flops onto the ground, finds a fallen apricot in the grass and eats it in one mouthful. 'Pat, this isn't a polite question but I really want to know. You and Jim— you're sort of like Keran and me—similar but different. So what brought you together?'

'You mean, apart from the obvious! Pass me one of those cots. If I tell you, will you quit being a disgrace to your intended profession and eat lunch when I make it?'

'Yes. I'm starving.'

'Well, ten years ago, in a heat-wave, my car broke down outside a garage in North Melbourne—I'm not kidding. I had just learned I was HIV pos, I was hopping mad, furious at having my life plans thwarted. So I verbally abused my poor car, until I realised that a lovely young man was quietly waiting for me to calm down. I watched him work on my car—my first lesson in patience. Me, planning to be a heart specialist, and nobody had ever shown me the meaning of patience. I didn't even know I liked dogs until I got to know Gertrude. We found Oscar here—a tiny pup, barely alive, dumped on the roadside. Look at him now, eh!'

The dogs rouse themselves, lick Patrick's face. 'Okay guys, up again. Mal, would you lend an arm, help a bloke up the last stretch? Thanks. That's a true kindness.'

After lunch, everyone has a rest; Patrick in his room, Gertrude and Oscar beneath the tankstand, Kerry and Malcolm under the low branches of the fir tree.

'So what are we going to do, Keran?'

No reply. Keran rakes her fingers through the soft pine-needles.

Mal stretches out on his back. 'It's your decision. I'll pay the bill but I'm not driving the Saab any more.'

'What a cop-out. Anyway, I feel like driving so that's one problem solved. We'll argue about the bill later.'

'Can't you at least admit this turned out all right?'

Kerry shrugs. 'Gay guys run good guest-houses, I'll say that much for them.'

'But you don't like them.'

'I like Jim. Pat's a pain, with his silly quotes. And he's a misogynist. You were as bad last night, you both ig-nored me. Without Jim, I wouldn't have got one word in.'

'Well, you usually get more words in than anybody, so it made a change.'

Kerry doesn't bother responding to that. They hear the phone ringing in the house. A few minutes later, Patrick calls from the end of the verandah: 'Jim says the engine's sounding beautiful. So. When you're ready?'

A sudden image of Patrick climbing the hill makes Malcolm call back: 'Pat, would you rather wait till it's cooler to drive us to town?'

'No probs, my car is air-conditioned. But thanks for the thought.'

Kerry stares at Mal as if he's been heat-struck. 'Why did you say that? If we waited till evening, we'd have the sun in our eyes all the way to the mountains.'

'So we *are* going west.' Malcolm grins.

'Well—the motel is still booked. I only cancelled one night, in case your lousy mood passed over.'

'My lousy mood? Talk about mirrors!'

'What mirrors?'

'Nothing. Tell you later. We shouldn't keep Pat waiting.'

'What's this sudden concern for Patrick? Don't tell me you're in love with him!' Keran laughs, and drops a fistful of pine-needles down the back of Mal's T-shirt.

Malcolm shakes his shirt inside out. Now how did it go? Love is not love which alters when it irritation finds? Near enough. He scrapes together a handful of needles, catches up with Kerry in the rose garden. 'Keran dearest, have you ever thought about how alike we are?'

Hide and Seek

Sarah Walker

'**C**oming out, ready or not!' Her sing-song voice swept through the house. In the dark, I sensed she was onto me.

I had known Lee Sheen for exactly twelve hours and had been in love with her for at least five. She was old—about seventeen—but living with her parents had made her even older, I think.

They were like that, the Sheens. They lived in Portsea all summer and Toorak in the winter. They had nothing in common with me.

Tell the truth; I don't even know why they were so rich. Luck; maybe. When you're fourteen, people's parents have money or they don't have money. You kind of take that for granted and don't bother asking why.

My place in Sydney was a flat in a ghastly red-brick block. There was no garden, no animals, no water for miles, unless you included Roselands swimming pool, which was more like a 50-metre coconut oil slick. My parents drove a Valiant and we ate at the League's Club on special occasions. I'd never seen an avocado or tasted olives. Pâté was something you put on the wall to fill holes.

But the Sheens' house in Portsea was a mansion. It was full of furniture that matched. They had no carpets, and they were the first people I'd met who thought that was a statement of style, not poverty. At lunch they ate biscuits with blue vein cheese or runny Camembert. They had salads with stuff in them I could only sniff suspiciously. At night there was always a barbecue.

My dad had moved to Melbourne when I was seven and he'd taken my older brother, Willie, with him. He'd married again—a nice lady who played the organ and sang 'nothing could be finer than tea with Carolina in the mo-or-orning ...' On holidays, I went to him.

My dad knew people. Rich people. Different people from the ones my mum knew. He had friends in high places. Everyone he knew had nice table manners and talked about things in the world, like politics and taxes and music. The people my mum knew talked about their feelings and other personal disasters.

That holiday, when I was fourteen, Dad took us to stay with the Sheens. 'They've got a house on the beach in Portsea,' he said. 'You kids'll love it.'

I wasn't sure about that. I didn't like meeting new people and I especially didn't like staying in their houses. You always felt like you were in the way. Like you were saying the wrong things, sitting in the wrong chair, eating too much. I didn't want to go and I said so. Dad said, 'Don't be silly, I work with Mr Sheen and they're a very nice family.'

Willie sang, 'Oh Mr Sheen, Oh Mr Sheen ...' I laughed.

When we got to Portsea Mrs Sheen kissed us all loudly. Mr Sheen shook my dad's hand and then Willie's.

'By gee, she looks like her father!' Mrs Sheen said, her fingers digging into my shoulders.

I glared at her dismally. I was going through one of those brief ten-year phases of hating my dad.

Lee wasn't there to meet us. I heard Mrs Sheen tell

Dad's wife, Carol, that she was staying at a friend's house. 'It's a girl who lives further down the street,' she said, adding in a loud aside, 'a very bad influence.'

We all ate dinner on the balcony, watching the light fade over the beach. I got eaten by mozzies and fell asleep to the tune of Neil Diamond's 'Hot August Night'. Before I went to bed, my dad gave me a boozy hug and said, 'This is what it's all about, kid.' He was sometimes hard to understand.

'Hey, you. Wakey, wakey, rise and shine, get up, get up, it's breakfast time!'

When I opened my eyes, a strange girl was standing at the end of my bed. Well, strictly speaking, it was her bed, but I was in it. It felt very early.

'C'mon, we're going sailing,' she said, 'and I'm under orders to be nice to you. So don't waste it, okay?'

Willie, in his army cot under the window, sprang to life, not caring that his pyjama pants weren't properly closed and his eyes were full of sleep. He'd met Lee before. 'Can I steer?' he asked.

Lee lent me an old wetsuit that was too small for her. She helped zip it up, although I didn't need help, and smiled at the way I looked. Her friend Anita was already on the catamaran, holding it steady off the shore.

'I've never sailed before,' I said.

'You're in good hands,' Lee answered.

For an hour I stretched along one of the cat's hulls, Willie like a book-end on the other. The spray drenched me and I lifted my face into it, listening to the foreign language Lee and Anita were speaking behind me. Tack. Gybe. Port. Starboard. They'd done this together before. Lying there, my fingers and toes stiff from keeping balance, I wondered why Anita was a bad influence. Less than an hour later, I had a pretty good idea.

The Sheens, Dad and Carol were all waiting on the beach when we got back. They'd set out rugs and deck chairs, baskets and brollies, wine and magazines.

'Good sail?' Mr Sheen asked Lee. He seemed only to speak in short sentences.

'Yeah, all right. A bit choppy,' Lee told him.

Mrs Sheen was sitting on a chair, shading the sun from her eyes. 'Get out of that wet gear and come straight back. No detours, Lee,' she ordered. Her tone embarrassed me and I turned away. Lee rolled her eyes.

In the change rooms I found a private corner. There was no one else there except Lee and Anita but I was shy about my body. I wrapped myself carefully in my towel before trying to peel the sticky wetsuit off my skin. It was awkward, to say the least. When I glanced around to see if the others were watching, I nearly choked on my own breath. Lee, whose breasts were full and tanned to a deep brown, had stripped off completely, while Anita sat on the bench and calmly smoked. I stared.

Lee laughed at me. 'Don't be so modest! We've all got the same bits.'

No, I thought, blushing to the roots, I haven't.

Inspired now, Lee leapt onto the bench beside Anita, her naked body still dripping, her pubic hair glistening with salt water. 'I'm an exhibitionist!' she sang. 'Round, round get around, I get around ... round, round, get around, I get around ... I get AROUND ...'

'Boom, boom, boom,' Anita added.

I couldn't look at her. I couldn't take my eyes off her. I was stuck. The unfamiliar wetsuit still clung to me like a straitjacket, my hands making a useless sawing motion as I tried to pinch the towel ends together and pull away the black rubber. Suddenly the song stopped. Lee stepped down off the bench.

'Silly girl,' she said, covering the ground between us in three long strides. Facing me, she grasped the two sides of the open wetsuit and laid me bare in one swift movement. Then she handed me a towel.

I squished a piece of pâté between my forefinger and thumb, then wiped it in the sand. The smell reminded me of how a pigeon looks when it gets run over. I looked around to see if anyone had noticed. My dad was crapping on about something to Mr Sheen, tossing back flies with one hand and the dregs of his beer with the other. Carol and Mrs Sheen were wearing big sun hats and blow-fly glasses. Only Lee was looking. She smiled. I smiled back. At that moment, though her back was turned to me, Anita's hand brushed Lee's brown thigh. There was nothing wrong with that, so why did it make me blush and pretend to see something more interesting on the horizon?

'Well, that's done us, I'd say,' said Mrs Sheen, clapping the sand out of her hands in a businesslike way.

Once one adult makes a move, the others always race each other to be seen doing the most packing-up. I sat where I was and watched Willie doing knee slides in the waves.

'I think you're a dreamer,' said Lee. I looked up. She was talking to me.

It wasn't my idea to play hide and seek. It was Lee's. She turned out all the lights and we waited for a sign. In the dark, I could hear Willie's faint breath.

'One, two, three ...'

Lee began to count. Adrenalin pumping, I let Willie beat me to the door. He escaped into the house, his silhouette dissolving into the pitch hallway. Before I could follow, a warm hand entrapped my wrist. Lee whispered, 'Stay here.'

She listened for a moment, perfectly still, then bent her head to kiss me. Just before her mouth reached me, she paused. 'Do you want me to do this?'

'Yes,' I said.

Though I couldn't see her, I felt the ripple of her smile and knew exactly what it looked like. She turned her head towards the door.

'Coming out, ready or not!' she sang. In the dark, I sensed she was onto me.

The Invitation

Robert Dessaix

Shocked wasn't quite the word for it. Outraged was more what Stan felt, and rattled, his mottled fish-mouth working to take in the humid air. And it was largely Marjorie's fault. He'd gone round to invite the man in for a drink on New Year's Eve purely as a courtesy, at Marjorie's insistence. So she was to blame. For the violet moons on his cheeks, the greyish scum on his lips and the trembling of his hands on the stainless-steel sink. Stan stuck out a knotted finger and bent a slat in the venetian blinds. There she was, kneeling down in the shade of the fence picking parsley, one doughy white arm flapping at flies. He let the slat snap back into place. He'd have something to say about this when she came in to make the sauce.

He'd never what you might call *taken* to the young fellow, not even at the start. And when Olive Hogg, who lived on the high side of the street and could see everything, had told him the new neighbour's name was Adam something-or-other and that he was the owner of a grand piano—Olive had seen it, beached legless and hugely black on the nature strip—Stan had started hacking back the jasmine quite viciously. 'Not a bad looker, either,' Olive said with a chuckle, stroking her nut-brown throat and cocking an eye at Stan from the footpath. Stan had lopped on in silence. Olive said things like that sometimes, her lipstick too crimson, her toenails garishly painted. Marjorie said she was a Catholic.

Giddy with heat and against his better judgement, Stan had gone over this particular afternoon and rung at the front door. Silence. He peered back at the street through the branches of the frangipani, reeling from its heavy scent and creamy flesh. No shuddering floor-boards, no shifting light on the mottled glass. Perhaps no one was home, although Stan could've sworn there was music playing somewhere, deep and lush. He decided to poke about. Petals squelched and oozed onto the flag-stones as he made his way round the side. He didn't nor-mally go round the side uninvited and had cut off his own backyard from the street by a lattice threaded with climbing roses. Not that Olive Hogg had ever taken the hint: several times she'd surprised him sweating in his singlet and shorts, jabbing at the onion-weed or mulching. If he heard her coming, he'd duck into his shed and push the door to, his chest heaving indignantly in the damp dark. Not a soul, not even Marjorie, had ever been inside Stan's shed.

He came briskly round the corner into his neighbour's backyard and stopped dead, blinded for a moment by a brilliant bolt of aqua light from the pool. Then he saw him: Adam was sitting facing him not two steps away in a striped canvas deck chair and he was stark bollocky naked. Black-haired and glistening and just lolling there. Stan blinked, astonished at the lightly haired limbs and torso smeared with oil, almost spreadeagled in the sag-ging chair, the wanton, slender ease, the furred belly and the hat. Cocked on his head was a red and white Santa hat. Speechless in the sodden, tangy air, welling with cellos, Stan felt his chest begin to heave.

And in the fluttering glare he suddenly saw Lennie again, Lennie Quade. Just a flash, but it was Lennie, down on the beach that summer years ago, half a lifetime ago or more, they'd been just boys, just bush for miles. "Let's go in starkers! he'd shouted—Lennie, not him, it was Lennie's idea—springing up and grinning and dragging off his shirt and his shorts and underpants, then swivelling round to stand tight and sinewy taunting him. Then he'd kicked him in the stomach playfully with one brown, smooth-skinned foot and said: 'Well, what are you waiting for?' and sprinted down the mirror of the sand into the waves and dived and disappeared and Stan had known he wanted to hit him hard, and be hit back, and hadn't known what else, if anything, he'd wanted, so he'd run in after him and leapt on him and wrestled him under and grabbed and jabbed and shoved and struck. And later, panting on the sand, he'd felt the kind of happiness that only comes with deep dissatisfaction.

'The leaves must make a mess,' Stan said eventually, startling himself. He flapped a hand towards the pool and looked up into the branches of the ghost-gums, scarcely stirring in the leaden heat.

Adam could barely hear him above the maddening cellos. 'The leaves? Yes, but I could hardly chop them down, could I? Look at those sheer white trunks! Aren't they magnificent?'

Magnificent? Words like that made Stan uncomfortable. 'Your azaleas are looking healthy,' he might say to a neighbour or, to Olive Hogg, 'I'd dust those cabbages, if I were you, you've got the moth.' Once, to the man on the corner, he'd said, 'Those marigolds make a nice show', but the man had only said 'Yes' and, if anything, had looked a bit put out, so Stan had been careful ever since of appearing too affected by what he saw.

'Anyway,' Adam was saying, 'we've got the pool-net.' And he gave the long pole a kick with his bare foot.

'Would you like a beer, Stan? Excuse me, I've gone native for the afternoon. Too hot to do anything else, really.' And Adam sat on, almost spectral in the hot blue glare. Still dazzled, Stan wanted to shade his eyes with his hand to look at him, but stopped himself. Adam pulled one knee up to his chest and dangled his other hand between his legs.

'I'll come another time,' said Stan.

'Was it about Simon, Stan?'

'No, no,' said Stan, and inwardly he reared. He didn't want his son's name said aloud here among this oiled, slim nakedness and scented air. 'I'll come back later.' And fled. Up the side, across the creamy, crushed carpet of petals and down the street, grazing his arm on the Graysons' privet but not caring. Queasy with hatred, he hurtled past Olive Hogg in her wide straw hat, picking at the roses, and Olive licked her sticky, crimson lips and looked back at the house with the cello music wafting up into the ghost-gums at the back and didn't say a word, but would, at what she would call a barely decent interval.

But now when Stan saw Marjorie coming up the steps onto the back verandah with the parsley in one hand and the scissors in the other, he found he didn't have any words for what he felt and so he darted up the hall, out the front door, round the side and over to his shed by the back fence. He bolted the door and sat hunched and seething, safe among his damp secrets.

'Well, *I* wouldn't have minded an eyeful of that one, I can tell you!' was what Olive Hogg had to say after Stan had told Marjorie and Marjorie had told her, cake-crumbs scattering all over her front.

'Oh, Olive, you can't mean that!' said Marjorie, and then thought of Jack Hogg and the slash where his right eye had been and his barrel body matted with grey hair and his hunted look. (Olive said it was the war.) Perhaps she did mean it. And more. Olive lit a cigarette and cackled. 'Olive, if you don't mind, not here, Stan's got a chest.'

'Oh, piffle, Marjorie, don't be so prim.' Why was the woman always so damned *wispy*? Stan this, Stan that, Stan the other thing. Olive preferred women who were *meatier*.

'No, but the thing is, Olive,' Marjorie cleared her throat of cake-crumbs, 'it's really Simon Stan's upset about. I mean, about Simon working in that bookshop of his. We're not sure if it's *wise* for Simon, you know, at his age, to ...' Marjorie fingered various phrases in her mind but the right one wouldn't come. The fact was that she didn't know any more what was wise or unwise, not after all the little humiliations she'd suffered, over a lifetime, really, ever since she was the mouse in some school play when she was six and forgot her lines.

'Oh, crap, Marjorie,' Olive snapped, blowing smoke quite wonderfully all over her, making her feel slightly light-headed. 'You're making a mountain out of a molehill. Simon hasn't said anything to you, has he? I mean, the man hasn't actually tried to *ravish* him in the stockroom or anything, has he?' Olive cackled again and crossed her legs. Ravishment had always tickled her fancy. 'Anyway, if you don't invite him, I won't come either. I don't care what he does in his backyard—or anywhere else, for that matter. I think he's gorgeous. Just *gorgeous*.' And she ground out her cigarette very purposefully, making tiny scrunching noises against the porcelain and blowing the last of the smoke out of the corner of her mouth across the tea things.

On the other side of the plaster wall, in a room smelling faintly of dirty socks and other pubescent things you couldn't quite put a name to, Simon lay on his bed and considered what his mother had just told Olive Hogg. After thoughtfully picking his nose, he ran a sweaty hand up under his shirt as he sorted through the implications. Once or twice he'd dreamt about Adam. Only once or twice, and he vaguely knew he shouldn't have at all, but he had. Nothing like *that*, or not that you could put your finger on—they were burglars in the dream and broke into houses together, except that once they got inside it always turned out to be Simon's own house and they ended up not stealing anything after all.

He'd known there was something different about Adam right from the start, when they'd first met at the corner shop and Adam had strolled back along the street with him. At first he'd wished he wouldn't, he never knew what to talk about with grown men, even his uncles, his mouth would go dry and his eyes would smart. But with Adam it had been easy. Adam had snatched at words he'd said and played with them, bouncing them back at him. He'd also liked his heavy black hair and brown wrists and chin but he knew he should never say that to anyone, not even Olive Hogg, and you could say practically anything to Olive Hogg.

Watering the hydrangeas one afternoon, Adam had asked him over the fence if he'd like to work in the bookshop he'd just opened, for a few weeks once school finished. Just unpacking books, sorting the shelves, wrapping, helping the less awkward customers—it could be fun. Simon had stared down at the footpath with a kind of dismayed elation and said he'd ask.

Stan hadn't taken to the idea at all. 'Don't know about that, son,' he'd said, giving the camellia a good squirt as he spoke. And Stan pictured the grand piano, the shampooed black hair, the socks that matched the shirts, the wide lips mouthing words you only read in books, echoing kinds of words, and he remembered the easy way he talked to Olive Hogg and even Marjorie, for that matter, the way he seemed to look them in the eye, and Stan said: 'What would you want to work in a bookshop for? No place for a young fellow like you.'

But Simon, while not wheedling, was sullenly insistent. Marjorie thought it was quite a step up and in the end got oddly terse with Stan, and Simon started in the shop. Opening the door in the mornings and walking into that silent, serried world of multicoloured rectangles was like entering a magic cave for Simon. How else could you describe it? There was something make-believe about it. You could almost hear the shelves rustling with pleasure and mischief and knowledge and passion. At the back of the shop, by the green-shaded lamp, stood Adam, like a wizard, full of words.

Marx, Zen, Afghanistan, Pushkin, poetry (people *bought* poetry), St Teresa, Chinese cooking, German dictionaries ... there seemed to be no end to the things people wanted to know and talk about. Olive Hogg popped in from time to time—a gardening guide, a murder mystery—nothing too *demanding*, as she liked to put it—and bantered with Adam and laughed and stood very close. Once, too, a tall young man who looked like a cricketer came in and kissed Adam. Simon looked away and thought briefly of groins. Not, he told himself, that he would want to kiss Adam. He wanted to kiss Anna van der Weel who was milky and Dutch and rubbed her breasts against him in the foxtrot. Sometimes in bed at night he'd even thought of kissing Olive Hogg, against a wall, sticky lips, sharp darting tongue, but mostly it was Anna van der Weel—biting her lobes and downy neck, and being licked and bitten, armpit, navel, and then he'd whisper slimy words into his pillow and shudder warmly, wetly into his sheets. He wondered what someone like Olive Hogg would say about the cricketer.

Trembling lightly on the papery air all day in the shop were sonatas, arias, fugues and quartets, rarely a symphony. One day, not long after the swimming-pool incident, just for a hoot, as he said, Adam put on a record rippling with outlandish words and pipings. And sang along, in a funny prancing way:

> For hell is just a properly PROPER
> As GREENWICH, or as BATH or JOPPA.

Simon felt as if he was trapped inside a maze, breathing hard. Anything could be around the next corner …

> … would see at her table, creamed and SET
> Marina sitting at her TOILETTE
> with eyelides closed as soft as the BREEZE
> that flows from the flowers on the INCENSE-trees.

When he went home for lunch that day he set the table, singing liltingly to himself.

> When Don Pasquito returned from the ROAD's end
> where vanilla-coloured ladies RIDE
> from Sevilla, his mantilla'd bride and YOUNG friend
> were forgetting their mentor and GUIDE.
> For a lady and her friend from le TOUQUET …

Stan looked as if he'd been hit with a plank. The violet moons began to smudge his cheeks. 'That's enough of that,' he snapped. 'It might be all right for your … mates up in the bookshop, but'—grey mouth working, oyster tongue slicking—'not in this house.' He slashed at the bread.

'Oh, Stan, really!' Marjorie kept her eyes on the trickle of tea into Stan's cup. She herself had been considered quite musical as a girl and had taken piano lessons for several years and, although it had never come to anything, not that you could name, she still felt those years of coaxing chords and melodies out of her clumsy fingers had given her something. What, exactly, she'd have been hard pressed to say.

Marjorie put the teapot down and took a stand. 'We still haven't invited Adam to our little do, Stan. I do think it would be better coming from you.' Stan buttered his bread in silence. 'Invite him, Stan, let's be neighbourly.' And they ate their sandwiches and drank their tea and gave no name to the heaviness settling sourly over the table.

When he went into the shop that Monday afternoon, Stan cast a yellowish eye around and felt pleased there seemed to be no one in the shop. Except Adam, who was up a ladder, stacking books, his head brushing right up against the mouldings in the ceiling. 'Hullo, Stan,' he said, flashing a smile. His teeth glinted up there in the half-dark and so did the little gold chain swinging on his wrist. Stan wandered over to the foot of the ladder. The polish on the fine calf-skin shoes pinched his nostrils. He looked up the length of Adam's body at the teeth and the chain. And in the depths of his begonia-potting, hedge-trimming mind something stirred. Grasping the ladder just at Adam's ankles, he saw in hectic colours Harry Carter. They'd dealt with Harry, shitty little bugger, slinking round the tables at the office party in a wig and knee-length frock, wiggling his bum and singing 'I'm just a girl who cain't say no', yes, well, they'd fixed fucking Harry, cain't say no, cain't say nothing at all now, Harry. Some of the boys said, 'Like a lift home, Harry? Pop in the car.' He'd got a lift all right, they'd ripped the little pervert's frock off, panties, stockings, Jim'd said, 'Are you going to say no to this, Harry?' and tried to stuff his pole up his bum while Wayne was throttling him, but he'd thrashed around and bitten and vomited chicken à la king all over Wayne and Jim, the filthy pansy cockgobbling mongrel, so they chucked him off the rocks into the surf and when he screamed and squawked, they laughed till they cacked themselves and spewed out filth into the watery darkness, fucking faggot, fucking queer, suck on some of that, ya poofter turd, and see how you like it ... and when he'd sucked and screamed and sucked and drowned, they'd all gone in for a bit of a splash in the raw. Jeez, officer, think our mate's been drowned, completely pissed—'course, we all were, been having a night out. The officer eyed the short black cocktail dress, put two and two together, probably, decent bloke, the officer, got the drift, smoothed things over.

In one swing Stan could've had the ladder over, backwards, Adam's head just scrambled eggs in matted hair among the English hardbacks. He gripped the wooden sides. 'Hullo, Dad.' In the doorway to the storeroom stood Simon, stock-still, just looking at him, like a cat.

'Simon, son. I didn't see you there.' And Stan swam back up again in eddies, blinking, and hated those cat's eyes in his son. 'I just dropped in to have a word with Adam here. About the thirty-first. You know.'

Adam said he'd certainly drop in.

Things came to a head, though, as Marjorie later told an avid Olive, when Simon came home one day and said

Adam had invited him to go to the theatre with him. 'And I said, "That sounds nice, dear. What is it?" And he said, "It's *The Nutcracker Suite*". You know, the ballet, it's on at the Royal. Well, Stan went quite peculiar, I really thought he was going to have one of his turns. He slammed down his knife and fork and said, "Right! That's it!" White as a sheet he was. And Simon went on eating his meal, didn't say a word, just stared at his plate. Then he looked up at *me* and I've never seen a look like that in his eyes before, Olive. A sort of hard, sneering, evil look. It frightened me. Then Stan said, "No boy of mine is going to any bloody ballet." He said it really slowly. "Especially," he said, "with a pervert."'

'A pervert!' Olive hooted, almost choking on her smoke. 'Oh, Marjorie, it makes him sound so *interesting*!'

'Yes, well, you haven't got any children, Olive. And then Simon just put down his knife and fork, got up and left the house. And then Stan got up and went out to his shed. Well, I couldn't eat a thing after that, of course, so practically the whole meal went into the tidy.'

Stan stewed for several days. Then, just as the light faded out of the sky on New Year's Eve and the whole yard filled with the scent of gardenias and daturas, Stan came out of his shed and set off up the street. As he went up the side, he could hear Marjorie clinking china and humming in the kitchen. When he got to Adam's house, he didn't bother going to the front door because there were lights in the backyard and he could hear splashing in the pool. The backyard was like a kaleidoscope, a jiggling maze of turquoise and yellow diamond shapes reflected from the pool, and every time the figure in the pool plunged or rolled, the walls, the trees, the fence, everything shimmered and danced like a cloud of butterflies. Stan put his hand up to shade his eyes from the glare. It was Adam in the pool, almost black against the dazzling aqua sheen. He raised an arm at Stan and swam over to the side, then hoisted himself out of the water, dark and lean and sparkling. 'Hullo, Stan,' he said, reaching for a towel, 'I was just thinking about getting ready to drop in on you.'

'Well, you needn't bother, my friend, now or any other time.'

'Pardon?' Adam stopped towelling himself.

'You're not welcome at our house. And Simon won't be going to the shop any more, either. You're not to have anything further to do with my son. Understand?'

Adam looked stung. He slung the towel over his shoulder. 'Now, look here, Stan—'

'No, *you* look here!' Stan stepped up to Adam and jabbed him in the chest. 'I know what you are and I won't have queers like you sniffing around my son. Just keep your filthy hands away from him.'

'And you keep yours off me!' And Adam pushed Stan sharply in the chest. And then a second time. Stan slid on the wet grass, gobbling and wheezing as he twisted backwards and down, cracking his head with a squishy pop against the tiles on the edge of the pool. Adam crouched, staring at him for a moment as he lay green-dappled and still by the water, then walked quickly off into the darkened house.

The water lapped, two voices murmured somewhere behind the glass doors, then Simon appeared in the doorway, just a towel wrapped around his waist. In the scissoring green half-light his body looked absurdly thin and bare. On thin, green legs he strode over to the edge of the pool, knelt and stared. Then very carefully he rolled the lumpish form into the water, picked up the pool-net on its long pole and pushed down with all his strength. A cicada was shrilling in a bush nearby. It went on and on. Inside Adam was saying something to someone on the telephone. 'You ... you toad-hearted bastard,' Simon whispered and began to cry.

Once all the fuss was over, at midnight or thereabouts, Marjorie had a remarkably peaceful night. She just sat alone in the dark among all the glinting Staffordshire and trays of untouched glasses and let the warm noises of other people's merriment drift in moistly from unseen backyards. Towards five, when the sky turned cucumber and in the space of minutes a ghostly grey-green garden formed outside the window, she got up and put an old Cole Porter record on and stood looking out, her hand at her throat. *Mm mm mm hmmmm ... da da dum, It brings back the sound ... of music so ten-der, It brings back a night ... of tropical splendour ...* Then she made a pot of tea and, just as the sun struck the tips of the pencil-pines along the back fence, she opened wide the door onto the back verandah, stood there a moment and went down the steps, across the lawn and up to the door of Stan's shed. She didn't bother rattling the padlock, she took the axe from the woodpile and with a sudden frenzied swing splintered the door. Then she swelled and swung again and again, gashing and smashing, until, spent and small once more, she could squeeze through into the shed. There in the greenish gloom she stood in a kind of calm rapture. All around her, above her, behind her, were rows and rows of African violets, like a choir-stall in a cathedral. Dozens of them, scores, hundreds. And as the apricot light of morning seeped down the walls from the pointed glass roof, the mauves, maroons and plums and purples began to glow in the damp darkness, swelling like half-heard chords, until she was surrounded by a rich cacophony of blood-blacks, porphyries, carmines, amethysts, lilacs and rubies, studding a water-fall of lushest green.

'Oh, Stan,' she whispered, in the stillness, 'it's beautiful. Thank you.'

Baked Beans

Dorothy Porter

I can pretend
  it's because
I don't like baked beans

I can pretend
  it's because
I ate too much last night

I can pretend
  it's because
I've got a period

I can pretend
  it's because
Martians have padlocked my mouth

I can't say
  it's because
she was so nice yesterday

I can't say
  it's because
she held me in her arms

I can't say
    it's because
her perfume makes me faint

I can't say
    it's because
she kissed me on the eyes

I can't say
    it's because
she's ignoring me today

And she's a teacher
And she's thirty-three
And she's married

And this is a school excursion
And my friends are whispering
And my parents would kill me
And my parents would kill her

But
    she told me
        it's all in my head

But
    she told me
        to grow up and forget it

But
    she told me
        to get a boyfriend

But
  she told me
    to leave her alone

Don't touch me   Don't touch me
  she said

And then
  she touched me

And then
  I closed my eyes

And then
  it happened

her arms   her smell   her voice
saying something into my neck

what did she say   what did she say?

Anyway
  she's not saying it today

Anyway
  she's not saying anything

Anyway
  she's not looking at me

Anyway
  I must eat my breakfast

And if I can't
And if I start crying
And if I throw this plate
    at the wall
        behind her beautiful head

I can pretend
   it's because
I don't like baked beans.

PE Lessons

Ian MacNeill

After the basketball had slapped Oak Boulez hard in the side of his face he became aware that Mr Antinopolous was saying something.

'What's our route then, Boulez?'

The guys were laughing.

'Next time pay attention, you slack poofter,' Oak heard the teacher mutter to the kids near by. The laughing stopped, except for Momtaj or 'Slaz' as Oak called him, because he was always bouncing around Mr Antinopolous' feet.

A fire now raged across his numbed bashed cheek.

Ants blew his whistle and yelled, 'Okay, guys!' And they were off.

'You all right?' Ki-Sang asked him as they broke into a trot together.

'Yeah. No. He hates me.'

'You should report him!' Hector Dimario said. 'I would.'

'Sure you would,' Oak said, wondering about it. Should he? *Could* he? 'Anyway he wouldn't have done it to you. It's me he hates.'

They jogged away from the change rooms and across the quadrangle. Some junior class was rioting on its teacher. Everyone looked to see who it was. Ants raised his eyebrows at the guys.

'They wouldn't do that if you were teaching them,

55

hey?' Momtaj said.

Oak felt vindicated when everyone groaned and said, 'Shut up, Taj, for shit's sake.'

They were heading for the gate—oh no, not a circuit of the school grounds. Mr Antinopolous had turned and was running backwards pretending to keep an eye on his charges. 'Keep up, Ki-Sang, we're not even out the gate yet,' he shouted.

Oak could see that Ants was looking at him to see how upset he was. 'For my next number I will take off my boob-tube and flash my tits,' he muttered to Ki-Sang, who began to giggle so much he had to stop.

'What'd he say? What'd he say?' Oak heard Hector yelling at Ki-Sang, as he broke out of the trot and began to run seriously to catch up with the class. 'What'd he say? Something about tits?'

'Stop talking and run, Dimario!' Ants yelled. And his eyes met Oak's and swerved away. He was worried.

As they ran out of the quadrangle and down the drive, Oak saw someone wave to him from the girls' gym class who were dragging gear across the sports area. He realised it was Aztaches and waved back.

'Looks like they've got to do hockey,' Ki said and at that moment Aztaches dropped the hockey stick for their benefit and clasped her face, pretending to be demented. That broke them up. They waved again and headed out the gate into the real world.

'Ants sure hates you. You should—' Hector began again but Oak broke into another run.

He felt elated now. When they were a little bit apart from Hector, he said to Ki, 'Oh God, look, what'd I tell you? How revolting. I wish Ants wouldn't do that. It'll cause car smashes.'

Ki-Sang had to stop running again. He bent over,

partly because he was laughing so much, partly in case Ants turned around again to yell at him.

'And hasn't he heard of waxing?' Oak called back over his shoulder.

'What'd he say? What'd he say?' he heard Hector demanding as he surged on.

He decided to catch up with the rest of the class and say something about Antspants flashing his big hairy tits. That'd pay him back. Anyway, who was the real poofter? Ants was always showering with the senior boys and walking around drying himself as they got changed. And what about that day he'd even turned up in bike shorts? 'Oh, sexy,' Oak had muttered and everyone had cracked up as Mr Antinopolous walked towards them, looking self-conscious. That was probably when Ants started to hate him. Then that plank Hector had said, 'Gees, Mr Antinopolous, you're flashing a bit of bulge there. You'd better not let the girls see, they don't like it.' Oak had imitated Hector's deep serious voice for their little group later and the girls had shrieked.

He was catching up. The training at night was paying off. And he was getting trimmer too. At least he could thank Ants for that. He hated him so much that he was determined to give him nothing he could pick on.

He pounded happily along with the others. He could probably beat a lot of them, even though they thought they were such great sportsmen. Anyway, he'd always been a good goal-keeper because his father used to make him stand between the goals to field the ball while he raced and dribbled about having fantasies about playing for Bolivia. *Oh look at this. What's going on here? This is incredible! It's Gomez, is he ...? Yes! A brilliant goal by Gomez. Bolivia wins the World Series.* Then he slowed down, he didn't want to get too close to Antspants.

He couldn't help noticing the way Ants tied his T-shirt around his neck. It was catching all the sweat running down. Ants was like some big shaggy dog. In a minute he'd shake his head and the guys near him would cop it. Probably no one would dare go, 'Oh yuk!' because once someone had and Ants had turned on him. 'Shut up! What are ya, some sort of pansy? It's just a bit of sweat.' He sure sweated a lot. 'Good healthy sweat,' he would say, wiping himself down with his rolled-up T and then chuck it into his office. He must have a million clean ones in there. Oak wondered who washed them all. He wasn't married, everyone knew that. Maybe his girlfriend ... He must drink a lot of beer to sweat like that. He probably went to the pub every night after training because he wasn't married and didn't have a girlfriend and he got lonely. Oak suddenly felt sorry for Ants and hoped he wouldn't turn into an alcoholic. He fell back to jog along with Ki and Hector.

Hector said, 'You're getting really good. I'll have to give up smoking.'

'You can't,' Ki said. 'You're hooked. I told you.'

'I'm going to give up when I'm twenty. Girls don't like it.'

'Some girls smoke.'

'Plenty of girls smoke.'

As they ran back past the sports area they watched the girls rushing about with the hockey sticks. Aztaches was concentrating hard. Pauline Huyn and Merrie Keleidaveto were leaning on their sticks, having a chat.

'Now twenty push-ups!' Ants ordered.

Everyone groaned but it was mostly a pretend groan. Oak had no trouble with twenty these days.

'Good, Boulez,' Mr Antinopolous said, standing over him. And Oak blushed furiously, with resentment, embarrassment, pride—he couldn't say.

'Don't crawl to me,' he muttered when Mr Antinopolous had moved away.

After dinner Oak went to his room and put Kreme de Kool in his walkman. He wondered if they were. Everyone said they were, you know ... gay. And he really liked the one they called Finni—the drummer. But everyone said everyone was. They even said Momtaj was because he looked a bit like Finni.

He became aware someone was behind him and looked around. It was his father.

'What homework are you studying? You're supposed to be doing your homework.'

'I'm just starting.'

His father sat down on his bed. 'How you going at school? You study hard? English is a very important subject. Are you learning good English? That Mrs Connell she said you don't pay enough attention.'

'Ms Connell. I don't have her this year. I'm paying attention. It's my best subject.'

'That's good. You do well in all your subjects, do what your teachers say, pay attention.'

'Da-ad!'

His father got so intense whenever school was mentioned. Oak dreaded every Parent/Teacher night. He sat at home, crouched over the TV as the hours dragged by, till at last the front door opened and his parents walked in.

'Now you're for it,' his sister would snicker. 'I tell him to behave!' she'd scream at their parents, as she ran from the room and he thundered down the hall after her.

Oak looked at his father. Dad obviously wasn't going to go away until he'd heard something more convincing.

'I'm doing okay at school, Dad, really. Except today Mr Antinopolous called me a poofter.'

As he watched his father's mouth fall open, Oak couldn't believe he'd said that.

'Ants was only joking,' he added quickly.

'What sort of a joke is that?' his father yelled, in Spanish of course.

'I was mucking up a bit. It was my fault. I bugged him.'

'What were you doing? What does he teach? Where does this guy live? I'm going around to see him.'

'Dad, no. You'll get me into trouble. It was P.E. I was mucking around a bit with Ki and Hector—you know, just talking, not listening, and it got on his nerves. He didn't mean it.'

'You weren't paying attention? Why weren't you paying attention?' His father stayed in Spanish; he was really upset. 'He shouldn't have called you that. I'm ringing the principal, that Mrs Stankovich.'

'Dad, you'll get me into bad trouble. Ants just lost his temper in front of the kids.' Oak wished he hadn't said that bit. He could see his father revving up. 'I won't do it again, I promise. I've learnt, I'm getting more mature. I was just acting like a kid.'

He could see that his father didn't know what to say now. 'Your mother works hard for you,' he muttered finally, after burning holes in Oak with his eyes. Then he left the room.

Oak felt like crying. What if his father did ring Stankovich? Mr Antinopolous would probably get into real trouble and get him into real trouble too. What if Stanks asked him in front of his father if he was a poofter? 'And *are* you a homosexual then Oak?' Oak could hear her saying it.

If only he'd been paying attention. If only Ants hadn't called him that. They were both to blame.

Oak opened his Physics book and tried to read the section on Refraction but he couldn't concentrate. Perhaps he should try to ring Mr Antinopolous and warn him. But what good would that do?

Why was it such a big deal?

He'd go and tell his father that it was just the same as saying 'wog'. All the guys called one another wogs, it was just a joke.

Mr Antinopolous was a wog too.

One Summer in the Land of Fez

Nadia Wheatley

I found myself driving past the house today. I didn't mean to. I was coming home from the supermarket, heading down the main road, and a petrol tanker had overturned just near that little park. Already cars were banked up and police were directing the traffic into the side street to the right. (Jamison Avenue. Remember?) Then left and into *our* street. (Do you know, I haven't been there since that last day?) For a moment I felt a blind panic—*how do I get out of this?*—but traffic was bumper-to-bumper, there was no way I could do a U-turn. No way I could avoid getting a long look at the front of the house. At our corner—wouldn't you know it?—there was another police officer, pointing left again, and so now I found myself crawling at snail's pace past the long side wall.

Nothing much seems to have changed there—outwardly, I mean. After all the hoo-ha we went through, the house is still sitting calmly on its corner, still looking the same, with its face of white-washed stone and its fringe of Virginia creeper. Inwardly, no doubt, it is inhabited by a yuppy couple. The whole neighbourhood is like that, these days. Odd to think that when we were there it was the pits. An area waiting for demolition by the Department of Main Roads, inhabited by squatters who had moved into the empty houses that the government had purchased. Odd to think that after all the trouble, the D.M.R. decided to put the tollway a kilo-metre over to the west. (I sometimes find myself wondering how my life would have turned out if they'd left us alone. Would I be driving home hot and bothered from the supermarket with the weekly shopping, wondering if I should have got some more shaving soap for Nick, crossing my fingers that my stepdaughter wouldn't complain about the type of milk I had purchased? Or would I be living still with you in the carefree Land of Fez?)

Arriving, I find Rowena undergoing a transformation. Last summer, she was a hundred per cent Mambo. Wore the same sort of T-shirts and baggy shorts as the skater-boys, and pump action basketball shoes that cost a fortune. I see them all in the op shop box as I carry the bags of groceries through the back door.

This year, she announces, she is going to be a hippy. She's been down to the city markets with her birthday money and has come home with a full white cotton skirt, a white Indian-style shirt, and a round white table-cloth of machine-lace.

'Being a hippy,' I tell her, 'is something that happens from the inside. It's a philosophy, not a fashion style. You can't just buy it.'

'And anyway,' her father chips in, 'with all this white you're going to look more like a nineteenth-century missionary.'

Rowena's face sets against us. Against me in particular. Though we've known each other for years, it is only a few months since I came to live here and she and I are still adjusting to our positions. She thinks I am boring and inflexible, bourgeois and naggy; under her influence, I think I am becoming so.

'I'm going to die,' she seems to be saying now.

Bloody little prima donna! One ounce of criticism and she's off the deep end.

But this time I have misjudged her. As she pulls out a paper bag and spills three familiar little discs onto the table, I am instantly transported back to the Land of Fez.

'I'm going to dye them,' Rowena had said.

Strange that this should happen today, after passing the house.

She scoops up the discs of dye powder, heads into the kitchen, pulls the soup-pot out of the cupboard, starts filling it with hot water.

'What do you think you're doing, Rowie?' Nick asks.

'I told you. I'm going to tie-dye all this stuff. The instructions say I've got to boil it up.'

'Not now, sweetheart,' Nick tells her. 'We've got ten people coming for dinner. I'll be needing all the space I can get.'

Yum. That means he's cooking something elaborate that will take him all afternoon. There is nothing I like more than being banished from the kitchen while Nick makes a feast. But Rowena doesn't look pleased at her exile.

'But Dad! I've got to wear this tonight! Zoe and I are going to a party!' She waves the white garments at him.

I watch them. Two faces clenched. The same dark curls, the same stubborn mouth. They are so alike. (And yet one of them loves me, and one does not.)

'Come on,' I tell Rowena. 'Bring the soup-pot and all your stuff out to the backyard. We'll make a fire in the barbecue and boil it up.'

Nick flaps his hands at the supermarket bags along the benches. 'Who's going to help me put all this away?'

I give him my best smile. 'No one!'

As the water heats, we twist rubber bands at intervals down the length of the skirt. 'Far easier than using string,' I tell Rowena, who has never done tie-dyeing before. She plans to have the skirt as an oceany sort of green with thin white bands of sea foam.

'Then you could re-use the green as the undercolour for the shirt,' I tell her. 'It'll be a whole lot paler, second time around. And when it's dry, you could tie little bubbles in the cloth with rubber bands and then do this deep pink over it. Oh and by the way—you need to throw a handful of cooking salt in the water. It helps make the colour fast.'

She gives me a look.

I could bite my tongue. When will I ever learn to shut up?

But it seems that she's not cross about me interfering; just curious.

'How on earth do *you* know all this stuff about dyeing?'

'Well,' I tell her, 'I once spent a summer in the Land of Fez.'

'Fez? Really? Is that in Arabia or somewhere?'

'Or somewhere,' I agree.

The Land of Fez was bordered on its two long sides by high walls of white washed stone. At the third boundary, backing onto the lane, was a fence of corrugated iron. The fourth side was the back section of the house itself. From the front, the place bore all the marks of abandonment. The two windows and the door were clad with thick pieces of sheet metal, and a large red and yellow sign announced:

PROPERTY OF THE
DEPARTMENT OF MAIN ROADS.
TRESPASSERS PROSECUTED.

That's what we were. Residential trespassers. We'd found a way in through the kitchen window and now lived in the big back room of the house. No electricity of course. Just candles. There was water, but only cold. And we did all our cooking on a barbecue we'd rigged up in the backyard. Not that we cooked every day of course. We were young enough to live mostly on love and Vegemite sandwiches. But once or twice a week we'd buy sausages for her and corn cobs for me (I was a vegetarian in those days) and have a feast.

That was how the idea of the dyeing began. One day, as I was scrounging for firewood through the rubble of one of the nearby houses that had already been demolished, I found the bowl of an old gas copper, disconnected from its fittings. We were great recyclers, though the word hadn't been invented yet. Anything we'd find, we'd also find a use for. 'What do you reckon?' I asked her.

She instantly went into witch-mode. Though she was a couple of years older than me, she could be really childish. Or child-like, I suppose I should say. Now she started muttering, *'Bubble bubble boil and trouble'* and other incantations over the copper bowl. *'When shall we two meet again?'* she went on. *'In thunder, lightning or in rain?'*

'Just remember I'm a vegetarian,' I warned her. 'No cooking up toads or newts or anything.'

'Okay,' she said, 'so we'll start by boiling up the sheets.'

'Not yet!' I warn Rowena as she goes to toss the skirt into the pot of green that has now reached a rolling boil. 'First wet it. Under the tap will do.'

'How come?'

'If you put it in dry, the colours tend to streak. You get a much more even effect if you wet the garment first.'

Of course, we built up our skill by trial and error. In the beginning, when we did the sheets, we were complete novices. Ended up with great undyed splodges on the material because we'd put it in the cauldron dry. And the colour was fairly raw. A sort of saffron, I remember, rather like a Buddhist monk's robes. Later, we tied bubbles in the cloth and re-dyed the sheets in a tub of pink and got the loveliest sunrise shade with concentric wheels of golden sun exploding. Then we got another set of sheets and toned from the pink through to a maroon and hung those up as our curtains. It was wonderful, waking up in the big back room of that house and seeing the sheets and curtains reflect the morning light as it shone in through the French doors that led to the garden.

We didn't use the front of the house at all, you see, didn't want to make ourselves conspicuous. Besides, it was scary in the two front rooms. The security patrols used to come around, twice or even three times a week, and shine their torches over the facade that looked onto the street. They'd rattle the big sheets of metal on the windows too—just to make sure no one had got in. Or to frighten those who had. We'd lie in bed in the back room, clutching each other. Luckily that wall at the side of the house was high enough to hide the barbecue, and the vegie garden we'd planted. But actually the patrols only seemed to bother about the front.

By now the skirt is ready and I show Rowena how to lift it with the kitchen tongs, then drop it quickly in a bucket and run it under the tap till the water goes clear.

Just as I'd promised, the remaining green dye is a lot paler now. She sets the pot back on the fire. Wets the white shirt and drops it in.

Meanwhile I wring out the skirt with my hands, hang it on the line. Rowena snips the bands and the breeze blows through, ruffling sea-green flounces and frilly white waves. My hands are green too, almost up to the elbows. Like old times.

In those days, of course, we were working with so many colours that our hands permanently took on the shade of khaki. And once we moved from the chemist-shop dyes to our own concoctions, well, I'm afraid we probably smelled a bit as well.

What did we make the dyes from?

Oh, stuff we used to collect on the demolition sites. And every day we'd go scrounging up and down the deserted railway line too. We tried both vegetable and mineral. Rusty bits of metal for red, powdered charcoal for a slatey grey colour, beetroot for purple and all sorts of weeds and leaves for greens and yellows. (I can see her now, her long red hair clinging damply to her face as she crouched over the cauldron, stirring a seething concoction of dock and nettle. 'In the olden days,' she said cheerfully, 'they would have burned me at the stake.')

It was a business, see. It was how we survived. She was on a teachers' college scholarship but I was still at school. There was no Austudy in those days, no young-and-homeless allowance for kids like me who didn't want to stay at home. And even though we lived in a squat, her scholarship wasn't enough to support the two of us. So we used to go around the op shops and buy old nighties and petticoats and singlets and shirts, bring them home and dye them, then she'd sell them to other kids at uni. Sometimes when we knew there was going to be a big Front Lawn meeting, I'd take the day off school, we'd rig up a bit of clothesline near the entrance to the quad and display the gear on hangers. That was our stall.

We did that for a month or so and then one day the Vice-Chancellor sent four of the little grey men—they were the internal security guards at the university—to make us pull it down. Of course, you can imagine what happened. We might have cowered in our bed from the night patrol but we weren't scared of little grey men in broad daylight.

We instantly sat down on the asphalt and started singing 'We Shall Not Be Moved'. A bloke from the Labor Club was addressing the meeting through the megaphone at the time—one of the draft resisters, his name was Dave Ransome—and he saw what was going on and called to everyone to come and join us. Within half a minute there must've been about three or four hundred of us, all sitting down around the clothesline, singing away. The four little grey men just stood at the centre looking stupid. Then one of them started conversing into his walkie-talkie, and in the end they went away.

'Another victory for people power!' Dave announced, and a girl called Jane took photos of us for the student newspaper.

After that, we were famous. Everyone at uni knew us. We got a sign for our stall, our own fashion label. We called ourselves 'The Tie-Dykes'.

My stepdaughter gasps and flinches back a fraction, then rubs at her arm, pretends she was hit by a splatter of boiling water. Pushes another log in the fire in order to look busy.

I wonder: Is it the word? Or the thing itself?

I have to admit that these days I don't feel quite right, saying it. Don't feel I am entitled to. It's one of those terms that belongs only inside the minority group. (Like my Koori friend Maureen can say 'blackfellas' as an expression of affection and respect; but I can't, without sounding racist.) In those days, however, it was *my* word, and I could do what I liked with it. Living inside a ghetto does confer certain privileges.

... But if it is the other? If Rowena recoiled from what I was? (What I still, to some degree, am?) Surely not. My stepdaughter is many things, but not homophobic. Indeed, I have sometimes found myself wondering about her and Zoe. Rowie and Zoe. The terrible twins. That's what we used to call them when they were younger. They were inseparable. And still are. (Is that why I am telling her this? To give her a lead-in for her own Coming Out story? Hardly! No, I'm afraid Rowena is as straight as a yard of pump-water—as my grandmother used to say about my hair.)

We are saved from our confusion by Nick, who appears carrying a bowl and two hunks of bread. 'Taste this,' he orders us, dipping the bread in some red concoction and poking it into our mouths, 'and tell me if I need to add more garlic.'

'No,' Rowena and I agree. 'It's divine as it is.'

And so is the shirt, now the pale green of new shoots. Rowena tongs it out, rinses, wrings, and is about to hang it on the line when I advise her to whip it in the dryer for ten minutes. It is not really orthodox but if she wants to do another layer over it, she'll have to hurry up. If she and Zoe are going out tonight.

'You two seem to be getting on like a house on fire,' Nick comments as Rowena disappears.

'Yes, we are.' For the first time, I seem to be telling Rowena something she wants to hear. Usually my conversation is limited to arguments about the milk supply. 'So buzz off, will you?'

Coming back, rinsing green out of the pot and heating up the water for the pink batch, Rowena asks, 'But why Fez?'

Ah ...

We saw it on television. At a friend's place, of course— without electricity, we didn't have a TV ourselves. It was just a documentary, about the Mysterious East, and among all the pyramids and camels there was a short segment on the cloth-dyers of a place called Fez.

We were rapt. The Fezians (as we called them) did it on such a giant scale. They had vats the size of a spa-tub, over fires which they fed with tree stumps. And into these vats they threw great lengths of cloth, which they stirred about with paddles. When the cloth was cooked, the Fezians lifted it out and festooned it from the drying lines that ran back and forth between the balconies of all the houses.

Of course, they dyed their material before the clothes were made. But otherwise, they were just like us.

Or we were like them. On a pygmy scale.

And yet it wasn't just the method that sucked us in but the notion of a whole town devoted simply to dyeing. Imagine (we thought) walking down those narrow cobbled lanes and looking up to see the loops of colour hanging from the air. Imagine the streets running with bright rivers when the vats were emptied out at the end of each batch.

(Did I mention that of course this was in the days of black and white television? So though we had seen the pictures, we had to fill in the palette for ourselves.)

Coming home that night, we lit a fire and mixed up some dye colours very thick, like paint, and used them to write THE LAND OF FEZ on the corrugated iron of the back fence. Then we opened a flagon of plonk, splashed a bit on the earth and the rest down our throats, and announced our secession from Australia.

'From now on, baby,' we told the government, 'you're on your own.'

We got a bit pissed that night and—okay, it's pretty obvious—we were rather stoned too. Well, it was the sixties after all. And I'm sure the inhabitants of the real Fez prefer hash to alcohol. Anyway, we lay beside the fire in the long grass beneath the lemon tree and watched a fingernail moon weave in and out through the branches as we made up the Five Laws:

#1 In the Land of Fez, it is always summer.

#2 In the Land of Fez, colour is our worship.

#3 In the Land of Fez, there are no cockroaches.

#4 In the Land of Fez, there is no persecution of people because of sexual choice.

#5 In the Land of Fez, squatters are allowed to live freely in D.M.R. houses.

I seem to remember that at some stage we took our clothes off and danced as we boiled up water and herbs in the copper. Then we gave each other a sponge bath.

We'd only just gone to bed when the guards came and rattled at the front, as if to mock our charter. 'That's *weird*,' we said, because they'd been there the night before. Usually we got a couple of nights of respite, between the intimidation.

And now it is time to put the shirt in for its second dip. We've twisted little bubbles all over it, so that tiny rings of green will be protected from the pink.

'This colour's gorgeous,' I tell Rowena. 'Should look great, with your dark hair.' The water is dusky and muted, like the inside of a camellia. I've always wondered why you're always able to get nicer dye colours in these powders than the dyes used in clothes or material that you buy. Of course, that's what we were capitalising on with our stall. People liked the colours of the clothes we sold. And even when the tie-dyeing craze really took off and lots of hippies were doing it, people still bought from us. Because by that time we were doing natural dyes, we had unique colours.

'How could you bear it?' Rowena asks.

I am far away. Bear what? Living with no electricity or anything? 'It was fun! Like a never-ending camping holiday. There was no washing up or housework, and we were never cold, even in the winter months, because we had the fire.'

'No, the terror,' she cuts in. 'The guys coming at night and bashing on the front door and shining their torches around. Weren't you scared they might break in and throw you out? Didn't you ever think of that?'

We weren't fools. Of course we expected that one day— one night I should say—the Land of Fez would be invaded. But we belonged to the Squatters' Union and the word was that it would be two or three years before the D.M.R. demolished our particular street. It seemed they'd run out of money for the moment and there were already rumours that instead of coming bang through our place, the planned route for the tollway was moving a bit towards the west.

'So why the constant harassment?' we asked down at S.U. headquarters a month or so later. Now we were getting two visits a night. Every night.

'Just hang in there,' the main S.U. girl advised us. 'It'll only be temporary. The guards must have had a personnel change.'

'More like a personality change,' we reckoned. In the past, they'd just been blokes doing their job. Flash flash, rattle rattle, and they were gone. Down the pub probably, to drink on the boss's time. But now they were like men with a mission. You'd think it was their private house that we were living in. Not, of course, that they really knew anyone was there. They were just trying it on. In case someone did move in.

And so, lulled by logic, we went home. Kept on as normal.

Well, not really. Now, we started doing all the dyeing in the daytime. Didn't like to light a fire at night.

Shirt's ready. This time I do the rinsing and wringing, while Rowie cleans out the pot for the third batch: 'Aegean Blue', it's called.

As she brings it to the boil, we cut open the rubber bands around the bubbles on the shirt. It's like Christmas morning.

'There! Oh, Rowie!' I think I'm as excited as she is. The pink over green has the most subtle effect.

I hang it while she wets the tablecloth, spools it holus-bolus into the pot of blue. She's decided just to do this one straight, she tells me. Then blushes, in case she's made a pun or something.

Somehow, when we gave up the fires at night, that's when we started to move apart. Before that we'd sat up late, talking or even singing, sometimes reading by the firelight. We were never bored.

But it wasn't the same, to sit inside around a candle.

Eating cold food, always cold food. Bloody Vegemite sandwiches again.

Or she'd bring home a pizza but it would always have salami on it. In the past, I would have just picked it off; but now, I reckoned she got salami just so she could eat the whole thing herself.

And apart from trying to interpret the meaning of the escalation of the night patrols, we ran out of conversation. We'd just sit there, with nothing to say.

Did I mention that by now I too was starting uni? I'd finished school in December, and by this stage it was nearly March. Orientation week was coming up. We planned a big stall—we could make a fortune, selling tie-dyed gear to all the freshers as they came in from the eastern suburbs, looking like dags—but somehow we couldn't seem to get the energy to build up the stock. Now I was to be a student, I would also get a living allowance and so we didn't really need to sell stuff in order to survive. In the end, we rigged up a short line in the Vice-Chancellor's courtyard and sold off all our remaining gear at bargain prices. (I think he must've known it was the end of the road for us, because he didn't even call the little grey men.)

... And it's possible too that beginning uni was for me a rite of passage which I wanted to do alone. Maybe I didn't want to start off with a partner. In the past, when I just used to go on occasional days, it was good to be there with her; but now I sometimes felt like one of the old married women you saw around the campus.

So all those things were reasons. And then there was the fear of course, the nightly stress we lived under. That would be enough to break any relationship. But I still reckon it was stopping the fires that really caused us to split.

By the end of April, it was starting to get cold in the Land of Fez.

That broke the First Law.

And once the eternal summer was over, the rest of the rules of our republic fell like the proverbial dominoes.

Nick is here again, this time asking Rowena to give him a hand carrying out the long table.

'How come?'

It seems we've set a fashion.

'I thought we'd have dinner out here—it'd be a pity to waste such a good fire. I'm doing seafood parcels anyway, so I can cook them on the coals instead of in the oven.'

'Do you want the chairs out too?' I offer but he waves no. There are enough steps and ledges for people to sit on. The table's just for the food.

But he does want me to set it.

I count out knives and forks for the people coming: Nick and me; Chris and Viv; Nick's new colleague and his wife (what're their names again?); Wayne and Helen from next door; Dev and Naajla; the Anastopouloses.

'You're sure you and Zoe don't want to stay for dinner?' I ask as Rowie helps with the serviettes. 'You could just eat and go on to your party.'

'Naah. We'll get a hamburger on the way. You guys always talk for too long before you eat.'

'Don't push her,' mutters Nick, who has only got twelve fish. 'Now, have you got enough money for the taxi home?'

'You've already asked me that three times,' Rowena complains. 'And look—blue's done!' She lifts out the tablecloth.

'You'd better do that in the dryer too,' I tell her, 'or you'll never be ready. Go on, off you scoot and put your gear on. I'll scrub the pot.'

'You sure?'

No wonder she's uncertain. Usually I am the greatest stickler for Cleaning Up After The Job Is Finished.

But I want some time alone, to think about the last part. And besides, rules are made to be broken.

As we quickly learned in the Land of Fez.

Of course, even before the summer ended, we had already broken Number 2. We had ceased to practise our religion of colour.

Looking back, I realise that when we stopped dyeing, we also stopped doing so many of the things that we enjoyed together. In the past, we'd had so much happiness exploring up and down the deserted railway line, scrounging through the demolition sites, as we collected wild fennel and nasturtiums and ragwort and the other plants to use for our dyes.

Now we didn't bother.

Nor did we bother to clean up after our patchy dinners. In the past, eating around the fire, we'd toss all the scraps in and I'm proud to say that we had an inner-city dwelling without cockroaches. But Law Number 3 broke down as soon as we started to eat in the house. Soon we had big ones, little ones, flying ones, German ones—the full urban roach invasion.

As for Law Number 4—No Persecution—well, I'm glad Rowie's not here for this bit.

One morning when we came out the back gate we found, scrawled under our Land of Fez sign, another bit of graffiti that said—well, unrepeatable things about lesbians.

'Do you think they mean us?' I asked.

'Who else?' she said.

After that, when we made love, I sort of felt as if someone sleazy knew. And so we more or less stopped.

We took to wearing clothes to bed, in case someone broke in and found us naked.

(Reaching out for you in the night, I encounter an armour of denim, a ridge of metal fly-studs, where before I used to find a feather-line enticing my fingers down and down into your softness. Oh my love.)

'Back again?' I ask brightly. 'You look gorgeous, Rowie!'

The pink-and-green flower shirt, and the green and white ocean skirt, black tights, Doc Martens, silver earrings ... and now a tablecloth of Greek blue to drape as a shawl.

She takes my hand. 'Thanks,' she says. 'Thanks for helping me. And for—you know ...' She tosses her hair back from her eyes. 'Can I ask what happened?'

I am ready now for the violation of Law Number 5. Can tell it with barely a tremor.

Well of course, one night they came not twice but once, and they came not to the front but to the back and they climbed the wall and stalked through the yard—we didn't even hear them. The first thing we knew was glass smashing as men came crashing through the French doors. So pointless. Breaking those doors. If they'd knocked, we'd have opened them. Did I say that the glass was coloured in sections at the top, really old and beautiful, with lozenges of red and gold? That's where the light used to shine through, in the morning.

Not that morning.

We tried to fight—not with fists, we weren't that stupid—but with words. Tried to get them to explain to us just what we were doing that interfered in any way with the D.M.R.'s plans. After all, if they weren't going to demolish the house for two or three years, why couldn't we live in it in the meantime?

And then I could hear chanting coming from outside. *'Homes, not tollways! Houses for the people!'* All those slogans. It turned out that the bailiffs had already evicted squatters from three local houses that morning and by now about fifty people from S.U. had gathered.

Not that it did us any good.

We were tossed out onto the street with just the clothes we were wearing. As if to mock us, the bastards got all the rest of our stuff—our glorious sheets and curtains, our clothing, even our lecture notes—and tossed it all onto our outdoor fireplace, poured petrol on it and burnt it.

By now the cops were there, to make sure the bailiffs weren't bothered by the demonstrators, and also the media, in the hope of gore and arrests. We were on TV that night, being carried out through the gate, and that was that.

The Squatters' Union people were really good, offered to help us find a new squat, but we'd had it. Both as far as squatting went and as a couple.

She went to her sister Jann's place for a few months and I moved into a big group house where Dave Ransome and some of the Labor Club people lived. And somehow I started to get more and more involved in the anti-Vietnam movement.

(And men. I don't say it. I don't have to say it.)

Yes, I do. I see the questions in Rowena's eyes. *'But how come ... And when ... And why?"*

Young people are so black-and-white. I used to be too. 'If you're not part of the solution, you're part of the problem.' That's what we used to write on walls. In my time you had to be either gay or straight; that's the sort of choice I faced. These days, I think it's not how you fuck that matters, but who you happen to love.

And if my choice seems like some sort of defection— well, just look at *her*! No backsliding there.

'*Here she comes*,' I murmur. We can see her through the open door into the house, kissing Nick hello, introducing him to Naajla, who's comparatively new on the scene.

'*What?*' Rowena sounds outraged. 'Why didn't you tell me?'

'But you always knew about Devlin.'

'I knew she was lesbian. But I didn't know about you and her.' She pauses, as if she is reassessing the whole story. 'You didn't say who it was.'

(I was telling it for me. Didn't have to name her.)

'So how come you're still friends?'

'Well, your mother and Nick are still friends and they used to be lovers.'

'Yeah, but ...'

But Dev is here now, juggling glasses and a champagne bottle, her eyes sparkling as she hears the end of my sentence. '*Who* used to be lovers? Is this the gossip corner?'

'None of your business,' I tease, as I kiss her hello, but Rowena lets the cat out of the bag.

'She was telling me about the Land of Fez.'

'What's that?' asks Naajla. She is wearing something long and bright that makes her look like a princess from the Arabian Nights.

'Just a place,' Dev explains, 'where we once spent a summer.'

'Oddly enough,' I tell her, 'I found myself driving past the house today. Nothing much seems to have changed ...'

Hamilton High School Speech

Cameron Sharp

n September 1991 I was invited to speak at the Hamilton High School seventy-fifth Anniversary Re-union as the 'representative' of the students of the seventies. Hamilton is a small town of ten thousand inhabitants in deepest western Victoria, surrounded by a mostly prosperous and almost inevitably conservative farming community. This is the speech and its story.

Hi. I'm going to try and keep this short. It's hot and Friday and when I went to Hamilton High School, which was from 1974 to 1979, the last thing, and I mean the very last thing I wanted to be doing on a hot Friday afternoon was sitting in this assembly hall, listening to a bunch of old boys and girls going on about how good it was in their day. Mind you, I don't know where you'd run off to have a smoke before getting the bus home, because they seem to have built on just about all the good hiding spots.

(A ripple of laughter from the back rows.)

That'll give you some idea that I was not always one to stay out of trouble. As a quick aside, there was a time when I pissed off one of my teachers and got chucked out of my English class. All I'd done was ask for some Durex—you know, sticky tape—to finish off some presentation but I found myself in the hall. For once I really didn't know what I'd done wrong. The vice principal believed me, to his credit, and went up to find out what had happened. I discovered a long time later that in England, where my teacher came from, Durex is the name they use for condoms.

(They liked me. I'd said 'pissed off' in front of the assembled dignitaries, talked about frangers and known what it was like to be on the wrong side of the law. Little did they suspect.)

And just a bit more history. In the seventies anyone who wanted to have a 'pash' would do it behind 'D' block at lunchtime.

(Quite a lot of muttering.)

Good. It's nice to know that some things don't change.

When your principal asked me to speak here today, he asked me to think about the school motto, 'I shall attain' what it meant to me, how Hamilton High School helped prepare me for when I left and what I have done since then. 'I shall attain.' I'll come back to that.

Briefly, I've been around the world a couple of times. I never ended up going to uni because I liked travelling and didn't see the point. I have worked as a typist, a street musician, a paper recycler, a baker and a truck driver, but most recently I have come back from Stockholm, Sweden's capital, where I have been helping to organise the Annual World Conference of the International Lesbian and Gay Association.

(I left space for a reaction. It was a good idea. There were close to one thousand people crammed into the hall. Seven hundred and fifty students, a hundred teachers, present and past, and the rest were locals who may well have had many of their 'best days' behind 'D' block. There is nothing to compare with a thousand jaws slamming onto a wooden floor, a thousand people whispering 'Did you hear that? Did he just say ...?' One elderly 'old boy' was fanning himself on stage behind me and gasping for breath. I tapped the microphone.)

I've got a bit more to say, actually, so as soon as you're ready, I'll carry on.

You may realise that being a young gay man here at Hamilton High School in the seventies was not a lot of fun. I would guess, from your reaction a second ago, that things probably haven't changed one heck of a lot. Which is a pity.

(My knees were shaking. There was an almost silence as a thousand people leaned forward to listen. I'd done it. Almost. Now I just had to get out of there alive.)

When I left here at the age of seventeen, I'd had six years of being terrified that, every time someone shouted 'poofter' across the yard, they had found out about me and that I was about to get my head bashed in (and possibly the rest of me).

If things haven't changed here in twelve years, then the world out there has. The world that is waiting for all of you when you finish here, whenever that may be, is the most amazing and fantastic place. And it doesn't matter if you don't get beyond Melbourne, or if you end up in Timbuktu. All that you need to know is that it will be very different and sometimes a bit scary. The time you spend here, and what you do with it, will sort out a lot about how you get on with life out there in the wider world.

'I shall attain.' Well, I didn't need to attain anything. I had it from the start, and what I had was being different.

Not just a bit different but different in a way that made my life really miserable because of all the people during my time at school who would pick on anyone who wasn't just like them. It's sad but I think they wasted six years here *not* attaining a bit of patience, a bit of respect for other people, a bit of common humanity. Not such a huge concept. It basically means that you try and get on with people.

So there I was. Different and surrounded by a bunch of people who thought they were my friends. People who did not in fact have any idea about who I really was, because I didn't know who I could trust and so I kept it hidden inside me until I could find people who I could trust. In the end I never told anyone but ended up hanging out in a small and pretty exciting group made up of all the other 'odd' kids. The thing we had in common was that we were all different in some way and that we knew there was safety in numbers.

Now, that was pretty frustrating, having to stay hidden, but I got on with school and did fairly well. Until everyone started going out with each other—Leanne and Steven, Andrea and Ricky. I could tell you about a few girlfriends your science teacher Mr Steer had, as we were in the same year here.

(Heads turned.)

But I won't.

(A little laughter welling up here and there. My knees had locked and I dared not move them.)

Try and imagine how hard it would be not to be able to fall in love when everyone around you is. Even the kids in my group of outsiders were falling in love but I couldn't. Because it was dangerous. Not just physically but because of the threat that I would be kicked out of home, ridiculed, hated, despised and a lot of other things besides. I was lucky, because I never learnt to hate. But I was bitter and angry and I took out that anger on everyone around me.

By the end of form five, as it was called in my time, I had been threatened with expulsion three times. These were not the sort of visits to the vice principal's office that could be laughed off, like a condom joke. I was an angry and frustrated and mixed up young man who did not respect his teachers and made it very, very obvious. I could do the work—that wasn't the problem. But in those days there were no school counsellors, no gay men or lesbians who you knew about or could talk to, nothing in the library to tell me about homosexuality—nothing good, that is. Hamilton was a very small town. In short, it was a bloody lonely time.

And I don't think it's a lot better now.

I got my HSC and left Hamilton and I have only been back to visit my mum and dad at Christmas every other year or so. Because once I left, I found that there was this world outside Hamilton that opened up to me. As well as all the sort of people who'd yell 'poofter' at you across the yard or the street or wherever, there were all these other people who accepted me for who I really was.

So, to be honest with you, I don't know what I attained here at high school. Perhaps Hamilton High taught me that I had to protest to survive. I have certainly been doing that since I left. I've chained myself to bulldozers on the Franklin River; I've marched against nuclear weapons; I worked for Greenpeace for four years.

Perhaps, from my difficult times here, I attained an insight into a world of people who do not have such an easy time. Since leaving, I have been involved in a number of HIV/AIDS support groups and have worked as a counsellor. Along with that, I have also been involved in social justice and human rights organisations.

Perhaps what I attained here was the need to question everything that was presented to me as part of the norm, because it wasn't a world I recognised easily, even as a boy.

What *you* attain is going to be as individual as you want it to be.

I know it's hot and a Friday but I'd like to add that it's actually great for me to be here. After all I've said, that might sound a bit odd but I came here today, more nervous than you can possibly imagine, for one reason. Years ago I sat in this hall, a very despairing young man who thought he was completely alone. If someone had stood up here on this stage and said to me, 'Hey it's okay. Just hang in there it'll all be okay,' then I would have been saved more pain and anguish than I care to remember.

I am here today because I *am* sitting out there in the hall. I could be your best mate, someone in the choir, the girl or boy who is sitting behind you in class. I could be anybody. And what you do with that idea will say a lot about what you are attaining here. If you leave this hall today and head out into that wider world unable to

cope with the idea of there being people who are different to you, if you continue to shout 'poofter' and bash up
kids because they're not as tough as you, then you're not
attaining anything.

But if you can accept that people have a right to
respect, to common decency and that thing I called
humanity—well I think you get the point.

'I shall attain.' What I hope is that you strive to attain
lives that let other people, in all their variety, teach you
just how great it can be to be challenged. About how
enjoyable it can be to think about things you've never
thought about before. I hope there'll be a million oppor-
tunities to respect the variety that goes into making up
our community and that you don't waste any of them.
Because it's not about whether or not someone is a
poofter or a leso.

It's about people. It's about you, me, him, her, them. Us.

Good luck.

(I couldn't move. I stood there and there was what
seemed like a very long silence before the place exploded
into applause. Up the back they were stomping their
feet, whistling. A number of students rose to their feet,
some in groups or rows, others in pairs, and a few brave
individuals by themselves. I was ready to cry.

Coming out in the place that I feared the most was
the bravest thing I think I have ever done.)

Next morning, shopping in the single main street, I was
accosted by a woman whose choice of clothing reflected
her undying support for the Australian Wool Corpor-
ation. She was smiling.

'My children haven't stopped talking about you. Well
done. It's just what this place needed, a good shot up the

backside. And about time. You see them leave, the young ones, because they don't think people here will understand them, and they're probably right, so they go to the cities.' She took a breath. 'But my kids have so many questions. I don't know what to say. I don't know what the answers are.'

I didn't know either. If there are any. But her kids were asking questions. That, at least, was a start.

The Suburban Spirit

Carol Jones

The first time Frank and Pamela mentioned moving to the suburbs, Sid didn't take them seriously. When they began traipsing through hallways haunted by men in suits bearing mobile phones, he just yawned and thought they'd grow out of it. He should have seen the signs—Pamela the hoarder organising a garage extravaganza, Frank the philosopher waxing lyrical about the pleasures of gardening. But Frank was like a lifestyle salesman who conceived grand new visions every other Monday. Why, just six months ago he had flown them all down to King Island to inspect a delicatessen that was for sale. Last year he'd subjected them to an entire week of strange pipe music, when he decided that they should all immigrate to South America and grow coffee beans.

After a while you learned not to take that sort of thing to heart or you'd be a nervous wreck. The suburban scheme had seemed like just another of Frank's visionary jaunts, until he and Pamela had walked into Sid's room one night (without knocking as usual) with foolish grins on their faces.

'Well, we've done it, Sid,' said Frank.

'Uh?' Sid had said, engrossed in his book.

'We've signed up.'

'For what?' he'd asked, growing slightly apprehensive. Frank and Pamela were rarely in such close accord. Yet

97

here they were, actually holding hands like honeymooners. Pamela sat next to him on the bed and ruffled his hair.

'The house. We've signed up on the house.'

Eh? Feelings of vague disquiet prickled the back of his neck. What house? He looked from Pamela's lipstick smile to Frank's pleased grin and decided that no, he hadn't accidentally stumbled into one of Frank's fairy tales.

'Have to buy a lawnmower,' said Frank. 'All that grass.'

Then he realised which house they meant. He remembered one particularly large hallway and a backyard with an expanse of grass and a sculptured mound in the middle, reminiscent of his local park. He remembered Pamela muttering about 'spaciousness' and Frank delirious about wattle birds. He also remembered how cold the house had been. Empty of furniture but full of ... something.

That house.

'Our house,' beamed Frank and Pamela.

'You could always move out,' offered his friend Dustin. They were hanging out at their usual haunt, a grungy cafe where everyone drank short blacks and picked at their focaccias.

'Oh, yeah? Where?'

'You could get a flat. We could get a flat,' said Dustin. 'All the guys could come over. There'd be no one to tell us to turn the music down or kick everyone out at one o'clock.'

He listened while Dustin painted a picture nearly as fabulous as the fantastical images he created for his art folio. That's how the two of them had got to be friends, when they discovered they were the only two in the art class who knew who Hieronymous Bosch was. They also felt a certain empathy over their parents' choice of names. Dustin's mother, Greta, was positive that Dustin had been conceived in the back of a panel van at the drive-in while Dustin Hoffman was doing his stuff in *Midnight Cowboy*. Sid was named after Sid Vicious. Pamela had once been a Sex Pistols fan back in the dark ages. It was hard to believe that someone in a Hilary hairdo once had an orange crewcut and a ring through her nose.

Anyway, since then they'd got drunk together, shared their first joint and their deepest fears. One night, sifting through a stack of Greta's '70s soft rock, Dustin had passed him a joint saying, 'You know, Sid, I always wished Greta had got around to producing me a brother. Don't have to any more, but.' Dustin had grinned and something deep inside Sid trembled in recognition.

Now Sid watched as Dustin waved his arms around. You could read his enthusiasm by the wildness of the arm waving. He gathered you into his dream by the sheer elemental force of his enthusiasm. His ideas were like tornadoes, catching you up and whirling you into other realms. Sid was sucked in every time.

'Or, you know, we could just move into a squat. We wouldn't need much stuff. Just a couple of mattresses on the floor and somewhere to put our books and paints. It'd be great. We could hang out all day, painting and talking and ...'

It was a romantic dream of freedom, far from the sub-urbs, far from Pamela and Frank. A wild dream of the two of them doing their own thing with no one to watch over them.

And then one of Dustin's wildly waving arms whacked Sid in the jaw and he knew it was just that ... A dream.

'Yeah, but what about school, Dust? What about money and all that stuff?' Frank and Pamela might be a drag on a guy's spirit of independence but they did supply the cash and a place to crash. In their better moments they could even be entertaining.

'Oh, yeah. Well, you know. We can work that out, Sid. If we've got no cash, we'll just have to look for a squat. There must be heaps of places out there, just waiting for a couple of likely lads like us to move in, eh, pal?'

Sid saw rows of crumbling terraces, doors hanging open by a hinge—beckoning them.

'An answer always crops up when you need one. Look, I gotta go. I gotta meet someone. See you at school tomorrow.' And Dustin was gone in a confident swirl of black overcoat, knocking cutlery off tables with his flowing scarf as he went.

Sixty days went fast. His school was finished for the year and he was finished with his school. His last year would be spent at a school where the guys majored in basketball and wearing their hats backwards and the girls were even more boring than the ones at his old school.

He waited for Dustin to bring up the subject of them getting a place together but nothing eventuated. After forty days and forty nights he realised that it wasn't going to happen. There would be no squat. No long nights of music and talk and ideas. He could go it alone, he supposed, but he knew deep down that he didn't have the courage or the vision. Dustin did but Dustin never seemed to stop long enough these days to get past, 'Hi, pal. What's happening?'

Nothing was happening. Nothing except the end of life as he knew it.

Frank bounced through the empty rooms of the house, giving Sid the grand tour.

'And here's your pad, Sid. You've got your own bathroom and look,' he gestured to a door, 'you even have your own entrance. You can get up to all sorts of hanky panky and Pamela and I won't even know.'

It seemed as though Frank had visions of his son luring girls up to his pad and seducing them with the persona of the mysterious artist. Frank had revelled in his day at uni as the dreamy philosopher (Pamela was one of his earliest victims and never quite escaped) and he obviously hoped Sid would follow in his footsteps. But when girls looked at Sid, they didn't see anything remotely mysterious. They usually didn't see him at all.

'Thanks, Frank. I'm sure it'll come in very handy.'

When Frank left him to play master of the manor, Sid sat on the carpet in the middle of his room and shivered. It was thirty degrees outside but in this room he shivered. It didn't augur well for his future in the suburbs, did it? He'd hated his room when he first saw it. Spacious, as Pamela had gushed, but it felt all wrong, as if he was trespassing on somebody else's territory.

The large window glared out at the grassy mound, squatting like a huge grave in the backyard. Now that he considered it further, the mound didn't look right either. Not like the careful mounds in parks, sculpted to reproduce urban parodies of grassy knolls or wooded hillocks. This mound looked like an accident, as if someone had just dumped a load of dirt and didn't know what to do with it, so they scattered some grass seed over the top and hoped the problem would go away.

He turned away from the window and flung himself down on the floor again. Lying sprawled out, the carpet berbering into his back, he closed his eyes and tried to drift, back to his cosy nook in the small city terrace, lined with the warmth of well-worn books picked up as he prowled second-hand stores, papered with his scribbles pinned to the wall and reverberating with the echoes of long conversations with his friend Dustin.

A breath of movement near his ear. A swish like curtains being closed and he opened his eyes wide, thinking that Pamela had snuck catfooted up on him. But no. Not a living soul.

He peered out at the mound again. Maybe it wouldn't look so forlorn if it had some green leafy things on it. He'd have to get Frank to work with a spade. That should cure him of this pastoral reverie he was indulging in.

Sid removed the old suit jacket he'd thrown on earlier. At least it wasn't so cold in here now. Perhaps the house was warming to him, even if he wasn't warming to it.

He dragged himself through the weeks before the new school year began, haunting his old territory whenever he could escape from the long list of chores Pamela had pinned to his door. Increasingly he felt like some unwanted wraith appearing at the least opportune times—when Dustin was on his way out or the rest of the gang had headed off on a jaunt for the day. When they did arrange to meet at the cinema or their cafe, it felt organised.

'Why don't you come over and see the new place?' he asked Dustin a few days before school started.

'Yeah, great idea, Sid. I'll pack my survival gear and

a tent and brave the dangers of the suburban jungle,' Dustin drawled.

Sid tried to camouflage the despair he felt with a laugh but the ruse didn't work. The small sound he emitted was pathetically close to a sob.

Sighing, Dustin said ruefully, 'Look, I'm sorry, pal. I know I haven't been out to check out your new place but the truth is ... I've been kinda hung up on this girl.'

Sid's sudden silence prompted some arm waving and an explanation. 'I haven't told you about it because—well, I felt like a dickhead actually. I hate feeling like a dickhead. Amethyst, that's the girl, she's been really pulling my strings but I think we've got it straightened out now. She's great.' His arms paused dramatically in mid-air. 'It's probably the old four-letter word.'

Amethyst. Amethyst. A jewel of a girl had been pulling Dustin's heartstrings, tying him to her side, keeping him all to herself. Sid wandered Brunswick Street with Dustin for another half hour but inside he'd already vanished back to the suburbs. Strangely, it seemed like safer territory now.

That night he searched his reflection in the bathroom mirror. He was seventeen and a half. According to popular image and society's rites of passage he was a man—almost.

He didn't feel like a man.

He felt insubstantial somehow. He kept waiting for the manhood thing to happen. Did it materialise overnight? Did you go to sleep a boy and wake up one morning knowing that you were a man? Or did it sneak up on you gradually, so that you exchanged your boy's identity item by item until one day you stood fully clothed as a man?

Hey, he didn't even look like a man. Yeah, there were a few wisps of hair he was carefully cultivating on his chin and his voice had lowered of its own accord years ago but he still felt the same inside as he did when his best friend Tom moved interstate when he was ten.

Young. Lost. Alone.

He was supposed to be too young, too new a life to have ghosts, yet the memories of past friendships haunted him. A whisper of shadowy movement behind him and almost, he thought he could see Tom's freckled face hovering in the mirror. Or was it Dustin's face he saw? Or just a reflection of his own unhappy spirit?

He wished that the face would smile. He longed for an arm thrown around his shoulders in camaraderie. Even a punch on the upper arm or a friendly headlock would do. Something. Anything.

'Frank, how old were you when you got hairs on your chest?' he asked nonchalantly, while Frank was engrossed in his current affairs.

Frank considered the question as deeply as if he'd been asked about the nature of God. Pamela glanced up from her tapestry, saying, 'I can tell you how old he was when he first got hairs in his *ears*. Thirty-nine and a half.'

'Thank you, Pamela. You do have a certain little way of making a man feel virile.'

Sid retreated to his room before the sniping turned into all out warfare. Obviously the honeymoon was over.

Throwing open the doors to his wardrobe, he rummaged blindly among the jumble of castoff clothes and priceless junk on the top shelf, searching for the small camphorwood box which contained his bits and pieces of memory. His fingers made contact with a glossy square of card, wedged between shelf and wall, and he pulled it down to see what he'd found.

A boy of about sixteen stood smiling out at him, the reflected sun from the swimming pool throwing arrows of light onto his bare legs. His arms were bent to flex his pecs. Showing off for the camera. Brown hair flopped over his forehead and a scattering of freckles peppered his nose. And then Sid noticed the trees in the background of the photo and he realised he was staring at a photograph of his own backyard.

The mound. Someone, sometime had filled a pool in.

He studied the boy in the photo more closely, this time noticing a slight uncertainty in those green eyes, as if his mouth posed for the camera—or the person behind the camera—while some other sadness lurked behind his eyes.

'I wonder what was eating you?' He surprised himself by asking the question aloud. There was something cosy about the boy's face. Sad, yet cosy. All was not right with his world either but you knew that he belonged. Perhaps to someone. At least to this house.

Sid wedged one corner of the photo under the frame of his mirror, so that the boy was staring straight out through the wall of windows to the mound. 'There. That's your kingdom. You're welcome to it.'

The radio beside the bed glowed 1.00 am when Sid's eyes snapped open. Moonlight drifted through the open curtains, silhouetting a slender figure in his room, moving towards him. 'Dustin?' he murmured blearily.

Maybe he was dreaming. Maybe there wasn't anyone there at all. Only wishful thinking personified. He sat up, peering more closely into the darkness. 'What are you doing here?'

'That's what I was going to ask you.' It wasn't Dustin's voice and he could see now that the boy didn't look like Dustin either, although there was definitely something familiar about him. Sid supposed he should feel scared. After all, some criminals began early and the stranger had obviously broken and entered his life. But what did he have that was worth stealing, apart from his collection of vintage Matchbox cars and his Abba LPs (all in original condition, complete with immaculate record sleeves)? It was a sure thing that nobody was after his virtue.

'How did you get in?' he asked.

'How do you think? I used a key. What are you doing in my room?' The intruder was close enough to the bedside now for his face to be illuminated by the digital clock. His freckles glowed an eerie green. It was the boy in the photo. A few years older but definitely the same boy.

'Just my luck,' Sid said. 'I'm lumbered with a previous occupant who sleepwalks. Listen, I think you're a bit confused. You don't live here any more, remember? You don't belong here.'

He supposed he'd have to wake the boy up, if necessary. But suddenly the intruder turned, opened the sliding glass doors to the yard and disappeared.

Talk about weird.

'I thought I heard voices coming from your room last night,' Pamela said next morning over breakfast. Frank winked at Sid from behind the Coco Pops.

'Must have been the radio,' Sid grunted.

Now why hadn't he told them about his nocturnal visitor? Or why hadn't he simply said, 'Oh, that must have been the strange guy in my room last night?' That would have shaken the sleep from their eyes.

But if he'd told them, it would've become their intruder, not *his* intruder. Shit! He must be getting pretty desperate if he needed to claim an intruder to fill his life. Wake up to yourself, Sid, he thought.

He went to bed that night almost hoping for another visitation, even while he knew he was being ridiculous. At least it'd be someone to talk to. Sid was famished for conversation. Even a chat about the probability of rain in Ethiopia would've been a pleasant diversion. So when a cool current of air whispered across his lips in the silent hours before dawn, he woke immediately with a soft gasp of anticipation. Once again the door was firmly closed against outsiders and yet he knew there was someone in the room. Observing him. Waiting for him.

'Hullo?' he ventured quietly.

'You're still here.' The boy spoke from the corner of the room by the row of cupboards.

'Uh huh.'

'This is my home. Who are you?' asked the boy.

'Sid. I'm Sid.' His visitor didn't offer his own name and Sid didn't ask. What were names for anyway? In the fantasies Sid liked to read, knowing a being's name bestowed a certain power over it, but in real life people handed out their names with careless abandon. For a few dollars at the airport your name could be emblazoned on a hundred small white cards while you waited. Names were no longer precious. Names couldn't hold people. They could slip out of your life leaving nothing but an empty name.

The boy moved closer to the bed where Sid sat, his knees tucked tightly to his chest. Tonight slivers of moonlight striped his visitor's face. He looked so natural, so comfortable, while Sid occupied such a small space that he seemed to be courting invisibility. Who was the intruder here?

The boy smiled—a smile of welcome—and sprawled at the foot of Sid's bed. 'I like your taste in books,' he said.

And then they talked. About books, about friendship, about life. But not, thank God, about the weather.

When Sid clawed his way from the cavern of sleep at 9.00 am, the boy was gone. A brief prick of loss threatened to become a gaping wound, until he caught sight of the mound outside his window. The boy would be back. Each night he would come soft-footed to Sid's room. They would whisper together in the long hours before dawn; closer than any brothers.

Frank was having an identity crisis. Wielding the shovel, with a ferocity that guaranteed a quick waning of enthusiasm, he and Pamela were attacking the mound.

'Don't!' yelled Sid from the window of his room.

Frank and Pamela looked up in surprise. 'We're just planting a few flowers, Sid. We're not burying any bodies.'

'Ah, yeah. Okay.' Flowers were all right, he supposed. Flowers weren't a desecration.

He must have had a strange expression on his face, because Frank and Pamela hovered in concern. 'Are you all right, Sid?'

'There used to be a pool here, you know. They filled it in. They wanted to forget it was here.'

Frank and Pamela exchanged glances. Frank coughed. 'Yeah, sorry we didn't tell you earlier, Sid. We thought you'd settle more happily if you didn't know. The house was such a bargain that we couldn't resist it.'

'We were going to tell you after you'd settled in.'

Pamela twisted her gardening gloves guiltily. 'Sorry.'

'For what?'

That night when the boy came, Sid was already awake. He stood by the window, watching the darkness of the backyard. The sliding glass door lay open—waiting.

Materialising from the shadows the boy approached, treading lightly across the dew soaked grass.

'I knew I had to stay,' he said. 'I knew you'd come back to me.' He stretched out his hand as if to touch Sid's face, then seemed to change his mind. Leaning forward, his lips brushed Sid's so lightly that he thought he might have imagined it.

Sid shivered.

'You'd better come in out of the cold,' said the boy.

They Have Captured Jean Moulin

Kerry Greenwood

The nurse had no time to scream as she was dragged into the scrub. A hard hand was slapped across her mouth and a voice growled in her ear.

'Please.'

She thrashed wildly, struggling in blind terror and striking as hard as she could. Venturing into the *maquis* was always dangerous. There were not only the Maquis, the Resistance fighters who took their name from the landscape, but also thieves and murderers and deserters lurking in the waist-high bushes.

Her hand encountered a shoulder, slipped down and touched something so surprising that she ceased to struggle for a moment. Whatever her attackers wanted with her, it was not rape.

'We need your clothes,' said an impatient female voice. 'Stop wriggling, you'll ladder your stockings.'

'Why do you need my clothes?'

'It's not as easy to steal a nurse's uniform as you'd think. Hurry. This is urgent!'

'Why?' asked the nurse again, obediently unbuttoning the straps that crisscrossed her breast. She could just see her attackers in the moonlight: three women. One dark, with a small gun which she held unwaveringly. One a farm woman with hands like shovels, dressed in an orderly's white coat. The last a thin pale girl, shivering in her underwear.

The nurse removed her uniform and received a skirt and jumper in exchange. 'Is it for France?' she asked. 'Are you going to kill me?'

'No, we are not going to kill you,' said the girl, dragging on the white wrapper and reaching round to secure the apron. 'And yes, it is for France.'

'Oh. What has happened?'

The peasant woman said in a husky Provençal undertone. 'The Gestapo have captured Jean Moulin.'

'Hush,' said the gun-bearer. 'No names. Thank you for the uniform. Go now and do not say a word about this. We may not survive but there are others who will remember.'

'I understand,' said the nurse. '*Merde*.'

She walked away into the *maquis*, uncomfortable in her donated clothes. She was late in meeting the army deserter who was her lover. He would be getting very hungry for the bread and cheese she was carrying.

'So, Marie-Ange,' said the newly made nurse, smoothing down her skirt. 'What now?'

Marie-Ange replaced the pistol in her skirt band. 'We go to the station,' she replied. 'I will tell you about it as we walk. Adjust your veil, Edmée—you are a nurse now, not a medical student. Isabelle, try to remember that you are a hospital orderly, not one who hauls cows around and sleeps in a midden. Stand up and don't slouch.'

Isabelle straightened her strong back and lifted her chin. She knew that she was a peasant and considered it an attribute of which she could be proud. Her strength had always been a delight to her. She did all the heavy work on the farm now that her father was dead and her brothers were gone, one into the army, another somewhere in the *maquis*.

'It is like this,' said Marie-Ange, brushing through the thorny bushes. Her voice rose clear and cool above the humming of the bottle-green flies disturbed by her passage. 'Moulin is the man whose code-name is Max. And Max knows everything. *Everything.* Since he was invested with the Croix de la Liberation, he has been in charge of us all. He knows the names, thecall-signs, the meeting places. And now Klaus Barbiehas him. The Butcher of Lyon can make anyone talk.'

'He will not talk,' said Isabelle heavily. 'I know he will not talk.'

'How do you know?'

'I've met him. A small man with greying hair, so ordinary that you would not look at him twice, except for his eyes. Ah, the eyes of Jean Moulin! Clear like water in a stream.'

'His beautiful eyes will not preserve him. The Gestapo will put them out.'

Isabelle winced. Marie-Ange, she remembered, was half-Irish and it was well known that the Irish had no tact. Isabelle herself was not given to sarcasm. She said exactly what she meant and if people chose to criticise her or take her up wrongly, that was their business. She knew what she was trying to say.

'Jean Moulin was the Prefect of Tours when the Germans came,' said Edmée, laying a hand on Marie-Ange's shoulder. 'They took him and tortured him. He thought he might break, so—'

'So he talked,' said Marie-Ange dismissively.

'So he cut his throat with a piece of broken glass.' Edmée's voice was matter-of-fact in the warm dusk. 'He survived but he would rather have died than betrayed what he knew. How much more does he know now?'

Marie-Ange took Edmée's hand and laid it against her own cheek for a moment. She kissed the palm and then let it drop.

'I hadn't heard that story. You could be right about him, then. Let me tell you what has happened.'

'Do you trust us?' asked Edmée.

Marie-Ange stopped and turned. Edmée and Isabelle gleamed in their white uniforms but she could be seen only as a darker figure against the dark.

'I trust Isabelle because she loves France,' she said, 'and because she has a brother in the Maquis.'

'And me?' asked Edmée.

Marie-Ange put a cool palm to the woman's throat, curving her fingers around the nape of her neck where the wheat-coloured hair was cut short and curled.

'I trust you because I love you,' she said simply. 'And because you love me.'

They stood still for a few moments in the *maquis*, in the dark. Then Marie-Ange took Edmée's hand and they followed Isabelle's white uniform along the path.

'Jean Moulin was taken to Barbie,' she began. 'Now I have met Barbie. A monster, he is a monster.' She clung to Edmée's hand and strong fingers clutched in sympathy. 'I know Barbie—and Moulin knew him too, perhaps. He drove Barbie into a fury.'

'How?'

'He pretended to cooperate, said he'd draw a plan of the Maquis camps. But instead he drew a caricature of Barbie, a really nasty sketch. Barbie beat him until he was nearly dead and ... you see his problem? He was to deliver Max to Paris but now Max cannot answer any questions. Barbie can't call in German doctors, for fear that they would report his rash action to Hitler. And so he has asked, very quietly, for a French medical team.

The two of you are supposed to keep Jean Moulin alive until he reaches Paris to be interrogated by Headquarters—but in fact we must get him off the train. At the sixth stop, remember that number. There are comrades waiting and the train will be stopped just before the town. We will alight with Max and then—away. Is that clear?'

'Yes. But how are we to distract the guard?'

'I will distract the guard.'

They had come to the road. Marie-Ange stopped and took off her flat shoes, hiding them under a bush. Leaning on Edmée's shoulder, she pulled on improbably high spiked heels and then tore off her scarf to release a cloud of scented, night-black hair. Edmée plunged both hands into it and pulled Marie-Ange's face down to hers.

'You would distract anyone,' she whispered. 'My beautiful Marie, my angel.'

Once, twice, she kissed the red lips. Then once more with a deep hunger that surprised them both. Marie-Ange released herself and smoothed down the skin-tight dress. She stepped out onto the hard surface of the highway.

'Behind me, good women.' Her voice floated back, light and careless. 'You should not be seen in such bad company as mine.'

Perrache was full of people. When Edmée and Isabelle came into the station, the crowd gave way to them: a neat Red Cross nurse with short blonde hair and the inquiring gaze of a child, accompanied by a big orderly in a white coat, a few years older, with soft brown eyes like a cow. They could hear ahead of them Marie-Ange's passage to the platform, gauging her progress by the hisses.

'Whore!' shrilled the women, clutching their babies

close. 'Traitor! When this war is over, we will shave your head.'

Edmée and Isabelle stepped over cases and avoided the panic flight of an escaped chicken as the train pulled in and the crowd began to move.

'Whore!'

Marie-Ange swung aside, tottering on her high heels, as a small boy spat at her. She arrived at the train unscathed, the two nurses close behind her. As she approached, the soldier on guard caught a whiff of Arpège and wondered deliriously what it would be like to kiss that smooth shoulder where the curve of the breast was just visible in the neckline of the black satin dress. She smiled dazzlingly and stepped closer. The soldier wondered whether he was going to faint.

Edmée and Isabelle ducked past her, flashing their passes at the guard. At the same moment Marie-Ange took his hand and allowed him to lift her abroad the train. Satin slid under his hands and he released her reluctantly. She smiled at him and stroked the back of a negligent hand across his cheek, setting his hair on end. His captain's glare sent him back onto the platform again, shaking.

The three women bustled forward through a carriage full of German officers. Marie-Ange, who was touching Edmée's back, felt her stiffen in every muscle as she saw the black uniforms of a group of SS. She gave her a gentle shove and they got through the carriage without incident.

The parlour car was empty except for a chair and a stretcher bed. A guard was standing at the door, half-asleep. He drooped over his rifle, straightening up when they approached. Someone was moaning, a low, tireless sound full of pain.

'We are the nurses,' said Edmée, using her few words of German. 'We will mind the prisoner. Has he spoken?'

'Nothing but groans, *Schwester*. I don't think he'll last but they want him alive, poor devil.'

Marie-Ange gestured the others forward and smiled at the soldier. 'And while they look after your prisoner, I will look after you,' she whispered softly, forcing him to lean closer and receive a waft of Arpège. 'See, I have a little present for you. A bottle of Cointreau, rarer than gold in wartime France.'

She smiled again and closed the door firmly on the two nurses.

'Edmée, it is indeed Jean Moulin,' Isabelle breathed, peeling back the army issue blanket. Edmée scanned the man's damaged face.

The jaw was probably broken, she decided, and the face so bruised that it seemed all one bruise. Nothing remained of the dapper Jean Moulin—*Jean qui rit*, the youngest Prefect in France—except the short greying hair still cut in a fashionable shape and the well-kept nails on the broken hands. Edmée stripped the covering from the naked body and felt over him for injuries. One arm broken, both hands injured and the ribs gave soggily under her fingers. He winced at her touch, although her hands were gentle and sure.

'Well?' hissed Isabelle. Edmée shook her head. New lines seemed to have been drawn on her smooth, young face.

'He ... he is not good. Give me the morphine. A whole phial.'

Click clack, click clack: the wheels turned. In the midst of her concerns Edmée was struck with a fierce, jealous pang, wondering what, exactly, Marie-Ange was doing to distract the guard. She could not cope with the thought and turned to assuage Jean Moulin's pain, since she could do nothing about her own. Edmée had wanted to be a doctor all her life. It was a discipline that transcended jealousy, perhaps even love.

'I wish I had learned more,' she said, frowning. 'But he has been beaten with a fist and kicked and flogged. This leg is broken and there are dozens of haematoma. I think he was dropped from a height—down steps, possibly, stone steps. Can you find a pulse, Isabelle?'

Who knew if the soldier was listening? He was outside the door, drinking Cointreau and kissing Marie-Ange. Edmée was willing to wager good money on the belief that, while kissing Marie-Ange, one could think about nothing else. She had fallen out of the sky into Edmée's arms, when Edmée had been alone. Edmée, who had thought herself dedicated to her profession like a nun. Edmée, who had never met a man she could desire.

She bit her lip. Isabelle said, 'His pulse is eighty-six but it falters. And he is very cold.'

'We must wait till the drug takes effect.'

Edmée ran a hand through her short hair and nibbled a fingernail. Time passed. With a jerk the train stopped at the first station. The guard made some joke in German and Marie-Ange laughed. Click clack, click clack, the train started again, taking Jean Moulin to Paris and an ignominious death.

'Edmée,' said Isabelle. The hand in hers had flexed and now the fingers tried to close. Jean Moulin opened eyes which seemed to have sunk into his swollen face. They were the same eyes that Isabelle had once known, clear as a stream, intelligent and kind, but now they were full of pain.

'Water,' he croaked and Edmée dripped a glucose solution into the broken mouth. Isabelle sat beside him, supporting his head on the slippery, glazed linen surface of her coat. Then she pulled the coat away and he lay on the soft curve of her breast, covered only with the often-washed fabric of her one good dress.

'Max,' whispered Edmée. 'Max, it's me, Mouse. We've come to rescue you, Max.'

The eyes seemed to focus. Jean Moulin swallowed and coughed, then whimpered at the jolt to his damaged ribs.

'Mouse?'

Edmée leaned closer. 'Yes, it's me. You're on a train going to Paris but we are going to rescue you.'

Again there was a nerve-shattering pause. A hand lifted to Edmée's cheek and touched it with icy fingers. She put up her own hand to cover it. Isabelle sobbed.

'Kill me,' said Jean Moulin with infinite effort and Isabelle stroked his hair, tears running down her cheeks.

'Kill you?' asked Edmée in horror. 'No! There are comrades waiting, Max. We have come to save you.'

And the door to the parlour car flew open. 'Spies,' roared the guard. 'Two Resistance spies. Are the French so weak that they are recruiting women now?' There was a service revolver in his hand and he was aiming it between Isabelle and Edmée. 'Stay where you are, *Liebling*,' he called into the corridor. 'There is a little problem but I shall be back directly.'

'A little problem?' Marie-Ange appeared, naked to the waist, hair floating like a cloud, and embraced the man from behind. 'Who's a big, brave soldier?' she teased and he tried to pull away.

'Leave me be, woman. I shall call the captain. Or perhaps I should just shoot them now.'

Edmée glared. Isabelle, with Jean Moulin in her arms,

said, 'Shoot then, Gestapo swine.'

'What did she say?' the guard asked Marie-Ange.

'She said "shoot" and called you a Gestapo swine. Although you are undoubtedly a swine, you are not Gestapo or I should have died rather than ever touch you. What's more, you are sleepy, aren't you, Marie's little pig? Pretty little piggy,' she chanted as he slumped gradually to the floor. 'That's Marie's nice, little, snoring piglet.'

She plucked the pistol out of his weakening grasp and dragged him over to the wall, placing the Cointreau bottle near his hand. When she pinched his cheek hard, he did not stir.

'He drank almost all of that heavily doctored liqueur,' she said, returning to the others. 'I thought it would never take effect. Germans have heads like teak.' She glanced down at her bare body, pulled up her dress and fastened it. 'Don't look at me like that, Edmée. This is war. You don't imagine that I am thinking about sex at a time like this, do you? Well now, how is Max?'

'See for yourself.'

Edmée stood aside from the stretcher, listing the injuries in a cool pathologist's voice. Marie-Ange went white.

Click clack: the train to Paris. The wheels turning, click clack.

The smell of Cointreau was heavy in the carriage and Isabelle swore that she would never drink it again. Against her body the head lay heavy but a little breath still puffed out the swollen lips. 'Oh, Jean Moulin, my dear,' Isabelle cried silently. 'I love you, Jean Moulin. I saw you once and I loved you. You were a hero and now we can't even rescue you. We have tried so hard but we cannot save you.'

'We must kill him,' said Marie-Ange. 'I have a gun.'

'No!' Edmée caught her by the wrist.

'Let go, Edmée. You must see that we cannot save him. If he came into your hospital like that, broken bones and who knows what internal injuries, what chance would your teachers give him?'

'Not much but some—some chance. I came here to save him. I came out of love and love doesn't murder.'

'Fool!' Marie-Ange tried to shake herself free but Edmée was stronger than she looked and clung like a monkey. 'You're still a child—you don't understand. Let me go, Edmée! I don't know how long the guard will sleep and the train is getting nearer to Paris by the minute. Listen, you can hear the wheels turning, eating the kilometres. You must let me go!'

Click clack, click clack. Outside the wheels turned but inside there was silence in the parlour car, where Edmée held Marie-Ange by the wrist, the guard chuckled in his dreams and Isabelle clasped Jean Moulin in her arms, cushioning him against the jolting of the train.

'Would you deliver him into the hands of the Gestapo?' Marie-Ange demanded furiously. 'Is that what you want? As long as he can still form words, they will make him speak.'

Edmée shook her head. 'I am a doctor, not an executioner.'

'Do you think I *want* to kill him? London sent me here into a war zone at the risk of many lives to save Jean Moulin.'

'That is not all that London said, is it?' Edmée did not relax her grip. She stared into the loved face, the soft mouth she desperately wanted to kiss. Marie-Ange's hair and her scent were making her dizzy with desire but she did not let go. 'What else did London tell you, Marie-Ange?'

'Let me go, '*Mie*, please.'

Edmée quivered at the intimate name. She was silent. The noise of the train made itself heard again. Click clack, click clack, click clack.

'They said ... London said ...' Marie-Ange choked over the words. 'They said, "Save him if you can. Kill him if you can't."'

'Yes,' said Edmée.

Click clack, click clack. No one had asked Isabelle's opinion but she was not interested in the argument. Jean Moulin's hand had closed on hers, his head rested comfortably on her bosom. Isabelle did not want anything else.

'Marie, don't shoot him. Please. I see that he must die. I see that. But let me do it my way. Morphine—I have enough to stop his heart.'

Marie-Ange leaned forward and embraced Edmée. The thin girl twisted with pain, grinding her teeth in agony, and Marie-Ange held her tight. Edmée dropped tears into the scented midnight hair.

'I love you; Edmée,' said Marie-Ange.

'I love you, Marie-Ange.'

Edmée found the syringe and filled it with more looted morphine. 'The needle will leave no mark among these bruises,' she told her lover. 'They will never discover that we killed him. Find me a vein, Isabelle, and—oh, Marie, look at him!'

Isabelle had turned Jean's head, very slowly and carefully, to reveal the jugular vein. The sight of that vulnerable, bruised throat was too much for Edmée.

'I can't do it,' she said and laid the syringe down.

'You must,' urged Marie-Ange.

'I would be a murderer,' said Edmée helplessly. 'I could never live with myself. I am a healer. I cannot do it.'

'No,' agreed Marie-Ange after a while. 'No, you can't.'

Click clack, click clack: the train to Paris. It stopped with a jerk at the fifth stop.

'At the next stop we are to leave the train. I will do it,' said Marie-Ange. She picked up the syringe.

'If you do,' said Edmée with aching sincerity, 'I cannot love you any more.'

"*Mie*, don't say that!'

'But it's true.' Edmée sat down heavily on the only chair. 'So I must say it.'

Click clack, click clack, click clack. The train started again. A tuneful baritone murmur in German indicated that the guard was singing in his sleep. The light in the parlour car suddenly seemed dim to Marie-Ange, standing balanced in her high heels with the syringe in her hand. They had to leave the train when it stopped next. What could she do? Edmée had a shattering truthfulness. But Jean Moulin must not come alive to Paris. And yet she loved Edmée in a way that no man could ever equal.

She walked to the stretcher and put her hand on Edmée's shoulder, brittle under her fingers like a bird's bones.

'Wait,' commanded Isabelle. 'Wait.' She stroked the bruised forehead and whispered, 'We are all your friends, Jean Moulin, my dear. We love you, dear Jean. It is all right to die now.'

'What are you saying, Isabelle?' cried Marie-Ange.

Tears ran down Isabelle's cheeks and wet the back of her work-hardened hand. 'He will not let go,' she explained patiently. 'To stop fighting would be to say that Barbie has won. He cannot die while he feels that it is Barbie who has murdered him. Even though he is not afraid of death.' She saw the blank faces of the other two women and added angrily, 'Speak, you! Speak to him, Edmée, Marie-Ange, you clever women.'

Click clack, click clack: the turning wheels. Edmée rose to her feet. Unnoticed, almost unaware, her hand came up to touch Marie-Ange's shoulder and to lay delicate fingers, feather light, on the man's chest where the bones sank into unnatural hollows. Her voice, when she spoke, was clear.

'Honoured Max, dear Max, it is your Mouse who speaks. You are surrounded by friends, by lovers. You can let go of life. We will watch you out of the world. Go now, Jean love. Do not make us kill you.'

'This is absurd,' exclaimed Marie-Ange, lifting the syringe. 'What are you trying to do—will him out of life by witchcraft? Five minutes more and we must get off the train or we are lost, all of us.'

Click clack, click clack. The train covered the ground, iron wheels loud in the dim carriage, and the guard sang 'Aufprés de ma blonde' in his drugged sleep. Isabelle, tears running down her face, said, 'I love him. Give him a little time.'

Imprisoned in pain, fiery as a cage of melted lead, Jean Moulin heard voices. Not the German of his torturers or the French of his school learning. They were women's voices, speaking in the cradle-tongue of the Langue D'Oc, and they said, 'You can die, Jean. You have not betrayed those who love you or the country of your childhood. You have defeated your enemies. It is safe, Jean. It is safe to die now.'

His agony had almost transcended feeling. He knew

that his body was destroyed. Inside his chest he heard the grate of shattered bone as it stabbed through something soft. He knew that death was a door and he longed to pass through it but pride would not allow him to be murdered.

Now pain stopped, as though it had been switched off like a light. He became aware of the soft breast on which he was lying, the peasant's strong arms, her cotton dress smelling of mint and wormwood and the milky, fresh scent of her skin. He could hear her heart beating under his cheek. He had heard that sound before somewhere.

Click clack, click clack, click clack.

'In two minutes we must be off this train,' swore Marie-Ange.

Edmée said to her sadly, 'No. We must stay with him. You see that we cannot leave him.'

'Are you mad?' Marie-Ange grabbed the girl by her shoulders and shook her, then kissed her mouth hard. 'Do you know what the Gestapo will do to you, Edmée?'

'Sleep,' crooned Isabelle in Provençal and the dying man whispered the child's word for mother.

'Maire,' said Jean Moulin and snuggled into her embrace. He turned his face a little into her breast and was still. Isabelle kissed the cold forehead and laid down the body that she had been supporting.

'Do not make so much noise,' she reproved, whispering as though he could hear and wake again to agony. 'Jean Moulin is dead.'

Stepping Stones

Caroline Macdonald

'**W**hen I was a girl,' Granma started.

My mother clasped her hand over her eyes, then peeked through her fingers at my father. I could see the broad smile behind the heel of her hand.

'My sister had a Greek boyfriend, and I decided I had to have one, too. We used to go to the Greek club. It wasn't a real club, just an upstairs bar where all the Greek boys went.'

My father was sitting a little apart from the rest of us, under a standard lamp, concentrating on a typescript. The light haloed his fine pale hair.

'We always called them boys. Really they were grown men with wives and families. None of the Greek women came to the club, of course. Just the Greek boys, and their young Aussie girlfriends.'

'Steve's hardly fresh from Athens,' my father said. It seemed he was paying some attention to us.

Steve was on the sofa next to my grandmother. Dark suit, white shirt, black hair, moustache, gleaming teeth, unbelievably gorgeous. His accent was expensive school. 'I can play the fruiterer as well as any Aussie comedian, if you want me to.'

My father smiled slightly and went back to his work.

'Steven,' Granma said. 'That was my boyfriend's name. Souteris was his Greek name. The first finger on his left hand was missing. He'd never tell me how it happened. But then his English wasn't good.'

'I'm second generation,' Steve said. 'I've tried to keep up a bit of the language.'

'I learned all the worst Greek curses,' Granma said. 'And how to say "I love you" and to recognise things like "I'm coming to your bed tonight".'

My mother shifted on her chair, glanced at me and picked up the wine bottle. 'How's everyone's glass?'

'It's amazing how much we girls liked going to that dreadful bar. It was a small city. In those days, anything exotic ...' She held out her glass to my mother. 'It's amazing, too, how things skate over your head when you're that young. One night I was getting off the bus and I saw Souteris waiting outside the tailor's. He looked straight through me. I couldn't understand why he was pretending to ignore me like that. A couple of seconds later I saw this woman coming out of the tailor shop. Souteris held out his hand. She gave him her pay packet. They didn't even speak to each other. He wouldn't say anything about it later.'

'His wife?' Steve said.

'She looked really old. In her blacks, and that bitter face. She was probably about twenty-eight.'

'Steve—can I give you some more wine?'

Steve took his attention from my grandmother and placed his empty glass on the low table. 'Regrettably, no. Some final phone calls about tomorrow's interview— may I use your study, sir?' He was standing, facing my father, who nodded briefly. 'So I'll say goodnight. Thank you for the terrific dinner.'

He did not forget to include me in his goodnights, taking my hand and looking into my face. That was the closest I ever got to him, and even though his eyes were so near to mine, I don't remember what colour they were. Then he was gone.

'He's an unbelievable flirt,' my mother said after a while.

'His mind's on political advancement,' my father said. 'He's practising his charm-school manner.'

'Well. I guess that puts me in my place.' My mother exchanged a glance with Granma.

My father was a member of parliament, rapidly advancing from the back benches. He'd started suggesting we might have to move to Canberra. Steve was his new gofer. Weekends back in Adelaide, Steve would be staying at our place from now on.

Granma finished her wine. 'Wouldn't it be better to have someone more permanent as an assistant?'

'I won't grieve when he moves on. We're all each other's stepping stones,' my father said. His eyes had already gone back to his reading. That was all right. I could talk to him later. Now I wanted to know more from Granma. I crossed to her sofa, took the space Steve had left. 'What happened about Souteris? Did you dump him straight away?'

I don't think my mother wanted more talk about Granma's teenage sex life. 'Time you were off to bed, Jasmine,' she said. I resented being packed off to bed at my age, particularly on a Saturday night; but it didn't seem worth making an issue of it. I stood up. Souteris would have to wait.

'See you, Jaz,' my father said. 'I'll come up and say goodnight to you later.'

That was good. I could talk to him then.

We had a two storeyed house—daytime rooms downstairs, bedrooms upstairs. There was a fence between the street and the front of the house, and in that space were frangipani trees, and clumps of daffodils in the spring as long as someone weeded out the ivy in the autumn. My parents' bedroom looked to the front; mine was at the back and looked down on the bricked courtyard. Beyond that was a building that used to be the stables last century. The people who had renovated the house, before we bought it, had turned the stables into a kind of artist's studio with huge skylights and added a small kitchen and a bathroom.

When Granma—my father's mother—came to live with us while her house was being remodelled, the idea was that she'd live in the stables. But with my father away five nights out of seven, it seemed the three of us were happy together in the house. My grandmother had the room next to mine. She was a night bird like me, and often I heard the faint electronic murmur of her PC when she worked late. She wrote articles for magazines—with a theme of 'when I was a girl' that disguised a commentary on here and now. My mother believed that she invented a lot of them.

In the meantime, the stables were Steve's on the weekend, it seemed.

I knew the sounds of the house so well. I heard the dishwasher start. My grandmother came up the stairs. She spent some time in the bathroom that she and I shared and then went into her room. My mother came up and I heard her door close. The house was quiet for a while. Then, below me, the back door opened. Through my window I saw Steve come out to the courtyard, close the door behind him, stretch, look up at the stars. I turned off my light so I could watch without him seeing me, but he didn't linger; he walked across the brick paving to the stables and went inside.

The door below me opened again and my father came

out. He sat at the courtyard table and lit a cigarette. I smiled. Poor guy, the nicotine patches weren't working. Now would be a good time to talk to him about my new life, for which I needed his support, permission, whatever. It would help to catch him at a vulnerable moment. We'd both know this was my reasoning, but it wouldn't matter. He always said I had the makings of a politician. This was praise from him.

I pulled on an extra jumper. The door to the stables opened, and Steve came out. He was bare to the waist, wearing only his suit paints. Narrow hips, muscled shoulders and chest. He sat down opposite my father. It was a clear and still night, but I knew it was very cold. As if my father was thinking the same thing, he reached across and brushed his fingers against Steve's chest. Both men stood and went into the stables.

I ran downstairs. Steve had papers for him to sign, I was thinking, final arrangements for tomorrow's TV interview. But when I let myself out to the courtyard, the stables were in darkness.

I didn't leave the courtyard. That was my mistake. I could have gone back to my room and seen as much. Or buried myself in bed and seen nothing.

I sat at the table. I sat for a long time, and I was so still that the courtyard lights—they were movement-activated—switched off. Long minutes passed while I shivered in dim starlight.

One light came on in the stables. I could see the outlines of Steve and my father through the glass door. My father was dressed. Steve wore a towel around his waist. I saw them move together into a long and sensual kiss. My reasons for waiting seemed insane and I stood up swiftly. Immediately the courtyard was floodlit. Their heads turned. I was discovered, indefensible.

I ran inside, up the stairs, into bed without taking off any clothes. I shook and squirmed and stayed awake for a long time. He would hate me.

In the morning I crept out of the silent house and went to early Mass. Afterwards there was choir practice. I was in the second row of the sopranos. In front of me, and to my left, was Fiona Bonnay, the leader of the altos. Her black hair shone and it was slicked to her small head. She never smiled, except sometimes at the end of a thundering *Dies Irae* or a poignant *Libera Me Domine* from the basses and I watched her, today, as usual, for that fleeting lift to her severe face.

I won't smile any more either, I decided. After practice I hung around, hoping Fiona Bonnay would invite me to have coffee with her, as she had once before. That was when she'd talked to me about the Church while I'd watched her soft eyebrows and her serious eyes that never left mine. Today, I could tell her about waiting last night to talk to my father, and what I'd seen. About my terror of seeing him again—the impossibility of our pretending nothing had happened, but what could we possibly say to each other?

I needed her to explain this mix of fears to me. I didn't know anyone else who could.

But she didn't suggest we have coffee. She nodded goodbye in a general sort of way, not focusing on me at all. She got into a green car waiting for her at the curb outside the church and moved close to the young man who was at the wheel. They drove away, and I had to go home.

My heart started pounding as I got closer to the house. But my father and Steve had gone. They'd left for an early afternoon flight to Canberra straight after the interview. I had a reprieve till next Saturday.

But that turned out to be one of those weekends when he didn't fly home. Extra committee work—unscheduled Caucus meetings—these things weren't unheard of. But what was unusual was that my mother arranged for time off work, and she flew to Canberra on Sunday night. I was left with Granma. It had been another Sunday choir practice with Fiona Bonnay disappearing.in the green car.

'Things might change round here,' Granma said. 'Your parents are considering a trial separation.'

This shouldn't have been a shock. I'd been thinking through this possibility. My mother had been saying things that should have prepared me, and it wasn't a surprise she'd got Granma to spell it out. However, minutes passed while I couldn't think of any words to say, but Granma wasn't waiting for an answer. She was back to what my mother called her girldays.

'There was a whole gang of us going to the Greek club for a while,' she said. 'There was a German girl—well, she wasn't a girl, really, she was a bit older than the rest of us. We liked her. She was generous. None of us had much money—I was always broke. Her name was Ursula and she was blonde and soft. One night we were both in the women's. It was a tiny place, the minimum I guess to comply with regulations. Ursula and I were squashed together by the hand basin. I remember her big soft breasts. She put her arms around me and told me I was beautiful and tried to kiss me.'

She stopped there, looking at me and making a rueful kind of face—wide eyes, stretched mouth. 'I pushed her away, and laughed and ran out of the women's. I knew nothing. I rushed back to our table. Eight or nine of us were there, more or less wayward with vodkas and ouzo.

"She tried to grab me!" I told everyone and added lots of detail. The boys guffawed and swelled up their muscles. The girls clutched at their boyfriends, pretending terror. I was centre stage.

'After a long time, Ursula came out of the women's. Our table sent a barrage of hoots and roars and so did the rest of the bar because the news got around so fast. Ursula ran out of the bar and she never came back. I didn't know where to find her. I wouldn't have known what to say to her, anyway.'

I pictured the girl stumbling down the dark stairs to the door, blinded by tears, into the empty provincial-city streets. Upstairs the bravura girls safe with their married boyfriends.

'She didn't even go to her table to get her handbag. One of the boys—Souteris I think—chucked it out of the window. I suppose it landed on the footpath. I don't know if she got it back.'

By now I knew that Granma had seen the events in the courtyard from her window that night. Her stories were never as random as they seemed.

'What happened to Souteris?'

'I met another bloke. Souteris was angry. He came after me with a screwdriver. I got back to my bedsitter in time to shut him out but he stayed all night outside my window, banging on the glass, shouting *poutana poutana* for hours. I was terrified.'

'Why didn't you call the police?'

'I didn't even consider it. I thought it was my fault. Something else to feel guilty about. I must have finally gone to sleep, because he wasn't there in the morning, and I thought I'd magnified the whole thing in my dreams. But there was a huge pile of cigarette butts outside my window. Two packets worth, at least.'

I hadn't seen my father since that night in the court-yard. We'd have to meet sooner or later. I still didn't know whether to pretend I'd seen nothing or whether to front up and say, 'I saw you and Steve.' But he knew that.

In the end, neither of us said anything about it. There was no need.

My parents separated. It was very discreet so that my father's political career would be safe. My mother and I shifted from the house with the stables to a cottage near her best friend Lil's place, and my grandmother went back to her refurbished house. I started going to Canberra every second month or so, to my father's place. We're still allies, as strong as ever. Perhaps stronger.

I stayed in the choir for a while, but I gave up the idea of joining the Church. I think it was just the music that I loved.

The Swing

Nigel Krauth

This guy has a great body. He's on a swing—a trapeze, I think—with the bar at his waist, arms straight beside his torso. He's lifting his own weight, so his upper arms are bulging and all his neck and stomach muscles are rigid. There's oil on his chest. I suppose it's oil. It gleams and looks like sweat.

If you turn over a few pages, there's this other guy—black, good body too. He's got a big black hard. He's holding it with gold-ringed fingers. His lips are a sort of sienna colour, red lipstick on black. His breasts are big, with coal-dark nipples. It doesn't look like they've used any oil on him.

The high school I went to was all boys. On the first day, if any new boy still had the maker's tag on his tie, he was dragged into the toilets and pushed into a cubicle. The tag was ripped off and then his head was forced into the toilet bowl and the chain pulled. He had to walk out into the playground, tagless and soaked, the water running off his head onto his new nylon shirt and pants.

'Tagging', it was called. It was an important ritual. It taught the value of trauma, of belonging, of continuity. We couldn't quite see all of that then but we did it just the same. Later I learnt that they also did it at the girls' school three suburbs away.

We lived in an outer suburb. The streets were still dirt and they had no street signs. Across the road from my family's house the bush began. It went on and on down to the reservoir. We did lots of things in the bush. One of our special places was a series of flat, exposed rocks, the kind the Aborigines left carvings on. There was a gouged outline of a big fish on one of these rocks. I don't know what kind of fish or sea creature it was meant to be. A small version of a whale, maybe, or a large version of a shark.

A group of us used to go there, three boys and two girls. We had just started primary school. We used to pull little twigs from the bushes. We used to take our pants off and poke the twigs into each other. The girls had more places for poking the twigs than the boys did. I still remember those little pink places, with the salty, earthy tang of the bush around us and the big outline of the unidentifiable fish.

We used to watch each other do poos too. Then we'd stick the twigs into the moist, curled mounds. We'd leave them there—looking like kadaitcha, I think now, like warding-off magic—and we'd go home to our suburban families to watch television and eat warmed-up frozen dinners. When we'd come back to the rocks, our poos would be gone. Later the Council put up street signs.

I remember a time playing with one of the girls from the fish rock under her parents' house. We were taking the pants off her dollies and looking at what they had underneath. Generally, it was smooth plastic. We were talking and giggling, I suppose. We could hear her mother walking around on the kitchen floorboards overhead. Then the kitchen floorboards went silent. I saw her mother's legs coming around the side of the house and I quickly started putting the pants back on the dolls. The mother bent down and came in under the house. She had a bread knife in her hand. She told me to go home and not come back again.

I raced out into the backyard and jumped over the fence. It was a tall fence. I don't know how I got over it so easily.

If you turn over a few more pages there's a part-Asian boy leaning against a kitchen bench. From the size of the sink in the bench, it seems the photograph was taken in a caravan. The boy is holding his dick right at the base, pushing his balls down—to make it look bigger, I suppose. He has no body hair at all.

Funny thing about magazine pictures, you can never tell how big the person is. What I'm looking at might be a four-foot tall boy with a six-inch dick or it might be a six-foot tall boy with a nine-inch dick. No matter how big he is, he's cut.

In my first year at university one of the lecturers threw a party. He had a terraced house in an inner-city street. There were women and men at the party but the lecturer was patting all the men on the bum and calling them 'Dear boy'.

I suppose we were men and women. We were seventeen and more. We stood on the balconies and in the doorways. The music reverberated against the rear facades and the back fences of the other terraced houses. The dope smoke floated over the dark, narrow backyards. Nobody danced. But the dance of the lecturer's hand on the bums of the men was memorable.

For a few months at university I had two girlfriends at the same time. One was short, plump and sweet. The other was tall, skinny and all, but she had terrific tits. I went to dinner with the short plump one at her house and met her parents. I liked her father. He drove an antique Riley and treated me (at some distance) as if I were a budding intellectual.

With the tall, skinny one, I got into the back of a car and we both undressed. Under her padded bra, there was nothing. I mean, there was something but it wasn't something that any man didn't have. I was on the look-out for padding after that.

Andy Appleton was the dumbest boy in class in primary school. But when it came to swimming carnivals, he was a hero. He could 'swim like a fish', as the headmaster put it at assembly. I suppose the school knew that Andy would never achieve intellectual honours in his future career but we depended on him to win pennants in swimming. He would leap to the boardwalk of the baths after winning a race, body streaming with water—I can still see that lithe water, held in his hair and in his eyelashes—and he would head for the change rooms, towelling his sleek skin. After winning, the penis would be sideways long, lying sleek, moulded by his wet Speedos.

This was the same pool where I had taken swimming lessons. I couldn't swim to save myself. The water was deep and dark. To dive from the blocks was a nightmare for me.

I gave up cricket in high school. I gave up being a part of the team. But joined another team, I suppose. At recess and lunchtime I stood with the non-cricket players beside the oval and talked about intellectual things. Like the real pronunciation of the word, 'yoghurt'. One of these boys, who always brought yoghurt and pig's trotters for his lunch, was also a ballet dancer. He regaled me with stories of how he had realised he was gay. The main story revolved around how he had been raped by two women when he was very young.

I often tried to imagine this.

The ballet dancer's friends were an eccentric bunch. I knew that and I didn't care if I was counted among them. One of them came to school at times with a band-aid stuck over his upper lip. This was to disguise the moustache he was sprouting. Another was always talking about Marx and Dostoyevski and how he one day intended to throw himself under a train to prove the reality of the world—or the reality of free will—I forget which. He later became a literary critic. I spent an evening at the ballet dancer's place, listening to his classical music and watching him pirouette. We ended up in the bathroom—he in the bath and me watching.

I felt I was at a crossroad.

Turn over the page and there's two guys on a diving-board up to the hilt. I don't like their faces. One has a turned-up nose. The other is pink-skinned and wussy-looking. But the setting is interesting. There's a pool and a backyard fence painted mission-brown. It looks like home but I guess the shot was taken in California.

On the next page it shows that one of these guys has an unusually bent dick. It goes sideways at the knob end.

When I was young, I discovered I could stand in front of the mirror naked and see myself as a boy. Then I could swing my genitals down, close my thighs on them and see myself as a girl.

I liked mirrors, shopfront windows, bus windows at night. I couldn't resist looking at myself.

I met a girl on the beach. I knew she was older than me, I suppose she knew how young I was. She lived quite close to the beach, further down where no one swam and the bush grew aggressively into the sandhills. She invited me to visit her house. We went together into the sandhills. We talked, lying on a sand dune together, and she said nice things about me. She faced me, with the deep space between her tits showing, with her bra strap held together by an obvious safety-pin.

What I felt was fear.

I was a lousy swimmer but it didn't stop me loving the beach. I surfed the shore breaks and left the deep water out the back for others. There was plenty to do on the beach without being a board-rider. Like watching girls, watching boys and scratching the sea-lice in your groin. One of the board-riders was Macca. He had the best tan of all of us. Macca showed his dick to any of the girls on the beach. He would see a couple of innocent-looking girls lying on their towels and he would attract their attention by calling or whistling. Then he would drag his Speedos down and give them a full view. Sometimes the girls would laugh. Sometimes they'd leave.

I could never work out whether it was seduction or intimidation that he intended.

Another beach. The kind where only fishermen go. Unpeopled sand, unridden surf erupting on glossy rocks, the protection of headlands and bush. An end to one of those desperately shared, private searches for a place to fuck.

'It's not in far,' I said. Pretending knowledge, pretending reassurance.

'It's not in at all,' he said.

There were three young men in the car. We were driving fast along a country road, seeing what the car could do. The ton, maybe? She was old, a Jaguar, leather upholstery, wooden dash. The needle climbed towards 100. That was miles per hour, on the old speedo. The vineyard hills hurtled by. The car purred loudly, guttural. She bottomed out on the long undulations in the road. Great old motor, but the suspension was wanting.

We thrilled ourselves with speed. Auto-erotic.

Another page in the mag, there's two guys and a girl. The guys are ball-deep. The guy on his back has the girl sitting on his face. His nose is in her backside. His tongue is probing. You can see the arch in her back, the delight in that glissando curve. You can see the Adam's apple of the other guy, chin raised, eyes closed, in plenty.

Such images. What is sensuality? Bodies don't have gender. They just have delight.

sucking a dick lychees and silk that's not it not quite it the smooth dryness the warmth difficult to word to harness the hardness and softness both the subtle resilience not blunt words not sharp words what sleek what insistent words elusive salt and velvet and sheen why do I think sheen why salt why velvet word-tease mouth-tease the odour too distinct like the texture explicit but always gliding away gliding away from words one word or more the shape of a mouth a mouth shaping to say its own shape

Open your mouth. Just that much.

I was fourteen, I recall, and it was night time. There were two girls on the swings in the park. Swinging high in their mini-skirts, with their shoes off. I thought I was in love with one of them. I had her name scratched all over my pencil box at school. They were sisters. My friend like the older one. 'Wouldn't she make your toes curl?' he said.

I had never thought about toes curling.

I missed the bus and hitched a ride home from school. On the Parkway, when my stop was coming up, I told the guy he could drop me at the corner. He seemed to be deaf. He kept on driving. He was wearing a dark suit. I watched my street go by. I saw the last line of houses and the last street before the Parkway swept on through the bush. I asked him again to stop. He pulled up at the side of the road. He leant over and put his hand on my knee. 'You've got a nice tan there,' he said.

I got out.

We drove along the coast, the woman and I, with a mattress in the back of the station wagon. We took our time. We found picturesque spots to stay—unknown beaches, deserted headlands. We cooked on open fires, drank wine under the stars. We made love on sand, on leaves and on the mattress. We made love in the surf too, and in rivers.

We had a good time.

I turn back to the guy on the trapeze. He still holds himself there, rigid. He still gleams. His penis, beneath the bar, isn't erect. It just sits, compact—without threat, but with promise. My partner looks at this picture too.

I know she likes it as much as I do.

Dumped

Merrilee Moss

(KIMBERLEY LIES ON AN UNMADE QUEENSIZE
BED STARING LISTLESSLY AT THE CEILING.)

Dumped. Pretty funny word really. Go on—laugh. Ha ha.
I'm not laughing. Too damn dumped to laugh. Too damn
dumped to read/sleep/open a can of soup/go out the front
door/play with myself/lift a toothbrush/care. (BIG
SIGH.) Too damn dumped to breathe.

dump, v.t. & n. 1. Shoot, deposit (rubbish);
let fall with a bump; send goods to foreign market for
sale at low price; drop down with a thud; land
(superfluous immigrants) in foreign country.
2. n. Dull blow, thud; heap of refuse.
3. v.t. chuck a lover/partner for ever and ever thereby
hurting them terribly and reducing their self-esteem to
zilch.

I'm not exactly suicidal, although the idea does have its
attractions. I am simply crazed out of my mind; self-
absorbed; filled with self-doubt, self-pity and self-hate.
But that's not all ... I am also extremely self-righteous.
After all, I am not the *dumper*. I am the *dumpee*. Thereby
lies the difference.

DUMPEE, innocent victim.
DUMPER, evil/bad/criminal/not to be spoken to or
invited to parties.

153

What does one *do* when one is dumped? What *can* one do when one is completely listless, filled with an overwhelming malaise (great word) and, through no fault of one's own, convinced one is nothing but a worthless worm? What can one do when one has so little sense of self that one keeps calling oneself *one*?

(ANOTHER BIG SIGH.)

What are my options? (RAISES ONE FINGER FOR EACH POINT.) I could wallow. Become completely self-obsessed. (No problem.) Seek help/therapy. (Too expensive.) Run to Mummy. (She'd blame me.) Phone an endless succession of friends. (She's out of town.) Soak endless tissues with snotty tears. (Can't use tissues—got to save the environment.) Starve. (No worries.) Chain smoke. (Too energetic.) Have a breakdown. (Define 'breakdown'.) Take a drink. (Too expensive.) Take up study. (Give me a break.) Take up jogging. (Do I look like Forrest Gump?) Have a nipple/eyebrow/belly-button/clitoris pierced. (What point adornment?) Hate myself. (Consider it done.) Hate my mother/my brother/the system/the homophobes/the 'other woman'/the dumper ...

Now there's an idea.

(ONE FIST JERKS INTO THE AIR.) *YES!*

I will focus on malicious intent/turn my anguish to seething fury/fill my veins with slime green bile. *YES!* (HER VOICE RAISES IN VOLUME.) Kill! Maim! Mutilate! Malign! Spill the blood of the treacherous traitor! Raise and use the unburied hatchet! Turn upon my tormentor with fists/feet/fingernails/heavy artillery!

(DESPONDENT SIGH.) If only I had the energy.

How can she be so cruel? Why doesn't she want me? Why? If there's nothing wrong with me—and I will assume for just one moment that there isn't—then clearly *she* has sinned terribly. She has rejected the glorious object of desire/lust/passion; turned upon the one that was loved/needed.

Where's the justice? Why isn't she in gaol? When will she be drawn and quartered/dipped in tar/hung from a tree/girder/rafter/light bulb at sunset? Surely when a dumping occurs, it is the duty of all loyal friends to immediately form a lynch mob/posse/wild, revenge-seeking mob of harpies to wreak havoc/knife her in the back/spit in her face/never speak to her again/bash her to a bloody pulp/at the very least to chastise her severely.

Where, oh where is the loyalty?

Where-air-air-air-air is luv? (I am in a musical.)

If I wasn't suffering from chronic lethargy, I'd go over there right now and scratch her car with my Swiss Army pocket knife/let her tyres down/hurl a rock through her window/phone up pizza delivery and have three thousand anchovy pizzas dumped/tipped/spewed at her doorstep.

Why do the rats always win? I am the honourable honest

monogamous faithful puppylike girl of anyone's dreams and yet I am left alone and lonely to age/rot/die of misery in the solitude of my empty and echoing room. It's so unfair and tragic.

Since childhood I have been gifted/tormented by a vivid, psychic and creative imagination. Call me a drama dyke, but I know I have an ability to see both absolute and possible truth in all its graphic, terrifying and gory detail. Even now I can see her rolling in ecstasy with her new true love.

(NARROWS HER EYES TO SLITS.)

Scene one. She is moaning with pleasure/ writhing/sweating/sighing/showing off every technique she knows/revelling in animal indulgence. But of course. That is the nature of falling in love. That is the nature of the new as contrasted so disastrously to the old. (Me.) She is enjoying a projected fantasy of desire rather than the reality of a real live person she has known for two whole years, three months and eleven days. (Not counting the last two weeks.)

Scene two. She is sucking toes, one by one. (May her new love have corns.)

Three. She is lying in bed her head nestled securely on her new love's breast. (May she snore like an ancient Anzac.)

Four. She is dancing at Girl Bar in her best black lace bra decorated with two hundred glimmering sequins stitched on lovingly and individually (by me, ignoring all risk of repetition injury and associated repercussions to my love life). She is dancing wildly. (She has tons of energy because her self-esteem has been inflated by seeing herself reflected three times her size in the eyes of her new love.) The music stops; she breathes hot air like fire onto her lover's lips. (I think I'm going to be sick. I can never go to Girl Bar again.)

(KIMBERLEY MOANS. SHE COVERS HER FACE WITH HER HANDS AND FLOPS DESPAIRINGLY INTO ANOTHER POSITION.)

I could take a bottle of Panadol (does it really work?); slit my wrists (messy); fit a vacuum hose from exhaust to window (if only I had a car); walk calmly into the sea, my cardigan weighed down with rocks (oh, Virginia); eat rat poison (do you know what that does to *rats*?); jump from a high building/mountain/hot air balloon; throw myself to the lions/crocodiles/piranhas; or choke on a peach.

But how could I be sure that *she* would find me/save me/feel responsible/suffer for the rest of her life?

The answer service. *Hi, Alex. It's me. Just rang to say I'm dying for love at around three this arvo. It's all your fault but don't worry. I hope you are happy. Have a good life. I'll be at the zoo, looking at the piranhas.*

A letter. Dear Alex. *You're probably wondering why you haven't heard from me for a few days. I'm sure you've been missing me terribly. I would have contacted you but I've been busy shopping for rope, rat poison, abseiling gear and a car. Would you mind if I* borrowed the hose from your vacuum cleaner for a few minutes on Friday? If you leave it on the front lawn, I'll pick it up but I won't be able to bring it back because I'll be dead. Sorry.

A poignant note by the body. My darling Alex. Wish you were here. But you're not. So I'm dead. Don't feel bad, even though it's your fault and everything.

How long are you officially allowed to wallow? How much time does one need before one is able to forget the fact that the dumper is doing disgusting things to another woman's body on a regular basis? Is there life after dumping? *That* is the question. Can one ever be friends with one's ex? That is another question.

If only she'd ring up right now. I'd hang up in her ear. Really hard. (SIGHS.) I wish she *would* ring. Then I could yell/argue/breathe heavily/tell her about my hurt/pain/angst/list all my grievances and cry a lot.

I bet she'll be bored out of her brain in a couple of days and come running back, begging for my forgiveness/body and attention. If she ever comes near me again, I'll ... I'll tell her to get fucked. I mean it. I'm never speaking to her again. I hereby vow and declare that I will never be friends with Alex. Ever. I mean it.

What if I run into them both *together*? I'll have a

seizure/vomit/faint/call the police/run under a truck/stare meaningfully into the distance.

If I wasn't having a severe depression, I'd go to the gym, get a body like Steffi Graf, lope gracefully and gorgeously down Brunswick Street with my new muscles and ...

(A GRUMBLING SOUND IS HEARD.)

Can you hear that? No, of course you can't. Only a dumpee can hear the molecules of air crashing overhead. Everyone else is too busy having a *life*.

(MORE GRUMBLING SOUNDS. SHE SITS UP SUDDENLY.)

Hey—that's not the sound of air molecules. That's my stomach! I'm starving! I could eat two poached eggs with hash browns, mushrooms, tomatoes, toast and caffe latte/a huge bowl of minestrone with grated parmesan/a fettucine funghi with Greek salad and garlic bread followed by chocolate mousse and ice-cream.

(KIMBERLEY STANDS UP, STRAIGHTENS THE BED.)

I think I'll ring one of my many friends. I think I'll clean the kitchen/walk the dog/have an orgasm/wash my hair/get a job/take my immensely adorable self out for a treat. I think I'll finish that sculpture I've been working on and plan a holiday.

(SHE HEADS FOR THE DOOR, THEN STOPS.)

What if she comes back now? Now that I've finished grieving. Now that I'm over it. Over Alex.

(TURNS AND GRINS.)

Alex who?

It's a Long Way from Oxford Street

John Lonie

Something's happened, like I'm jumping out of my skin which is pretty weird, all things considered. I got bashed last Monday, see. My head's still sore, my face is all puffed up, my arm feels like it's been wrenched free and put back in the wrong way. Since I got home from the hospital, Mum's been giving me painkillers which are supposed to make me sleep but I'm so wide awake it's like I've been asleep all my life till now. You'd think my dick'd lay off, seeing as I'm black and blue all over. I try to think of other things but that doesn't seem to work. Dicks, they rule your life, don't they? They give you away. Them and your eyes. I read that in the olden days, you could be forced to go to a special doctor who'd show you photographs of naked men and women. And he could tell which one you liked most because there was this machine that could measure the pupils of your eyes if they expanded which, when you like something, they do. 'His eyes widened' is how they say it in novels, like 'Dave walked into the room and Mike's eyes widened' except they never say that. It's always 'Dave walked into the room and Susan's eyes widened'—in our school library at least. Still, no matter what's happened, I'm glad I live now and not then.

I haven't been to school since Monday and the doc says I probably won't be able to go back for at least a week. But things are all up in the air. Mum and Dad went feral because the principal said he didn't know what was worse, me being bashed or what happened on the weekend, which is the cause of all the trouble. Like it was my fault. Then Mum had this big argument with the principal because she rang the cops. He reckoned it was a matter for the school to deal with which is what Dad reckoned too.

Jarrod's been standing out in the cold behind a tree on the footpath over the street, looking towards our house like I might go out and say, 'Hi Jarrod' as if nothing's happened. He doesn't think I can see him but I can. He was there when I woke up. Maybe he's been there all night.

Jarrod's tall and blond while I'm short and dark, on account of Dad's family's from Mauritius which is French mixed with Indian and just about anything that washed up on the shore there. I take after him rather than Mum who's Australian. Jarrod's eyes are so blue you want to swim in them. But mostly it's his smile that hooked me. 'He smiled and my eyes widened.' I've wondered lots of times why it's so special, like what are the facts of my not being able to take my eyes off his smile? Why his smile and not the smile of Jason Albello or Nick Forward or any of the others? The facts of Jarrod's smile are that his mouth is wide and his lips are sort of thick and shaped like a heart and when he smiles, his face goes from being cruel to being so soft and happy that you want to laugh and touch him. You know there's a good guy somewhere inside.

It was about a year ago, middle of year ten, when I saw Jarrod the first time. He'd just come down from Queensland with his folks to live in Sydney and he was smiling because Brother Gillespie made a joke about him fitting in with us Mexicans—Mexican because we're south of the border. 'Whaddyou lookin' at?' he said to me and stopped smiling, like I was looking at him naked which I wasn't, but I guess he must've thought I was. I couldn't help it. I was agape which is just the word. In English, agape means agape which is a bit dickwit but according to Brother Gillespie, it's really a Greek word and in Greek it means love. I sort of mumbled, real dumb, but I guess when I look back on it, I must've been in love with him from that moment.

Brother Gillespie put him right where I could see him so I could daydream about what it would be like to kiss the nape of his neck where his hair was starting to curl. The teachers get shitty with me about daydreaming. 'You with us, Michael Renouf?' they say. They can't say much more because I get okay marks in everything except maths where I'm near the bottom which really pisses Gillespie off, like I'm deliberately not trying. Which is like saying I'm *deliberately* into guys and not girls. Not that anyone knew that—well, not for sure that is—even though some of the guys called me faggot for a while last year. They call anybody faggot. It doesn't mean anything except if you really are one and you don't want them to know because sure as look at you, they'd beat the shit out of you just for being gay. You should hear them talk about it, how they're going into Oxford Street to bash the queers. Who's a hero? Not me, no way. It's a long way from Oxford Street and I'm all by myself out here.

About a week later, Gillespie moved Jarrod to where I couldn't see him properly. Made me so damn pissed off. I got into trouble that day. Sometimes I can't hold my temper, see. Irrational, unreasonable, no sense to it. It's not a bad thing like I do it all the time. Just sometimes. I can't help it. Things just get too much, y'know? The school counsellor tries to counsel me but I sit there and just make it all up and agree with whatever she says. She thinks I've come a long way until the next time I go a bit berserk. Lucky for me I do go berserk, not that it saved me last Monday. Except it probably did stop them murdering me. My elder bother says it would have been manslaughter, not murder because I'm a faggot and even then they would've gotten off because they're so young. Dad clipped his ear but still, you can see why I've had to be so low-profile around here.

Those guys might know for sure now I'm gay but there's lots they don't know—things about me, things about Jarrod. I got to know Jarrod before anybody else because he was lousy at maths like me and Gillespie used to keep us back. We weren't the only ones but because the others were the dickheads and we were both good at other subjects and not at maths, we were singled out and placed together. There was some hope for us. Me and Jarrod'd walk to the station together and catch the same train and talk. He was new and didn't know many people. Though when footy season came he began to play and because he was so good at it, suddenly he was friends with everybody, particularly the guys. But till then, he was mine. He came to my place a couple of times because it turned out he lived one station past mine and one day it just happened. He's the first guy I ever had sex with. The only guy actually.

He started it. The first time we just wanked but after that we took off all our clothes and he'd get on top of me and come like that. He said it was because he didn't know any girls yet which I never believed for one second. I could tell by his eyes. Of course. Besides, you know when someone's really into something and he was into having sex with me. Me, I was in heaven and when he was pumping away and moaning on top of me, I could hear his heart beating faster and faster and I'd kiss his neck and that would drive him wild. We did it lots of times, actually. One time we were just lying together after we'd come, my arms around his back and his head resting against mine, I swear I was never so happy in all my life and I said, 'I love you, Jarrod.' 'Don't be such a fucken dickhead,' he said, real pissed off with me, and got up.

Then footy season came and he didn't come round as much. After a bit, he stopped coming round altogether. One Saturday night, at the movies at Parramatta with Mum and Dad and my brothers and sisters, I saw him with a girl. He saw me and said hi, like you'd say it to anyone who was just a friend and not special. The girl, she had braces on her teeth and held onto him like he was her own private property. The film was *Batman* but I didn't follow it. When the lights came up, Mum looks at me and says, 'What's wrong with your eyes?' And says to Dad I might have to have my eyes tested for glasses. And when we got home, one of my brothers said something or did something and I went berserk and Dad gave me one of his clips behind the ears. They never hurt and he always looks like he wants to cry after he's done it. Well I cried, all damn night I reckon I cried but not from Dad's clip on the ear. So in the morning Mum went on and on about me needing glasses. I told her I was coming to Mass with her and Dad said, 'In that case, there must be something wrong with him.'

I sat up the back by myself and I prayed. I said, 'God, you go on about love all the time and what a good thing love is. Well I love Jarrod and that can't be a bad thing but now I feel like shit. So please help me to love girls instead.'

Nothing happened. The big zero. I looked at girls at the station and I like talking to them but that's all. I just went on feeling sore about Jarrod and seeing him at school every day made it worse. I even asked a girl out to the school dance but it was hopeless. You ask your dick, 'What do you like?' And my dick's always said back to me, 'I like guys.' That's the way God made me. Though you should see what bits of the Bible say about homosexuals. 'But this is the way I feel,' I keep saying to God, 'so how come if you make me who I am, it's supposed to be bad? How come it's so wrong for a guy to fall in love with a guy?'

I never got an answer until last weekend at the school retreat and I reckon this must be why I'm jumping out of my skin. It was at this place past Pittwater which you get to by ferry. Pretty uncool, lots of huts with double bunks and a big meeting room, but the bush is excellent. I kept to myself and went walking a lot. I even found a hut where I could be all by myself the first night, though people from university came the second night.

There were lots of speakers with talks like Christian Virtues, the Role of Women, the Role of Satan, why there's bad in the world. Mostly it was pretty boring. I sat by the window so I could look out. Jarrod sat near me, like he was trying to be friends again but I still couldn't look at him without wanting us to make love and it still hurt. So while he sat next to me, I wasn't there, not really. I was right inside myself, a long way away where I reckon it was just about the safest place to be, with him sitting there next to me.

So I wasn't taking much notice when this young guy gets up to speak. He starts talking about having begun to study for the priesthood and the demands that it made and how he studied the Bible and all the great religious masters. And I'm wondering, what's this guy trying to say? Then suddenly he's saying it. He starts to read from the Bible and it's that bit from St Paul where he says guys definitely should not get off with guys. The Book of Romans ... 'Here we go again,' I think and start to turn off. Brother Gillespie's looking smug and so's the guy who's running the whole thing, a priest though he wasn't dressed like a priest.

Then the guy says that Paul was also against women and that he thought slavery was okay so why pick out just the bits against guys being with guys? What is important is that Jesus Christ said nothing about homosexuality and that His greatest command to us was that we must love.

I could tell that this is definitely not what the top guy was expecting and Gillespie was looking real nervous, because now the guy is saying that he stopped studying for the priesthood because he realised he was gay and that the had learnt from his study of the Bible and knew in his soul that the command to love was meant for gay men and women as well as for heterosexual people. And that the laws and attitudes against gays were the laws and attitudes of human beings who are all capable of being wrong.

It was so totally silent you could hear people breathing. No one clapped. I stared at him like I was agape in the dickwit sense. Did I hear all this? I looked at Jarrod and soon as he wouldn't look back at me, I knew that guy had said it all. Suddenly the top cheese guy gets up, no 'thank you' or anything and says it's lunch break and Jarrod clears off like I had AIDS or I'd kissed him on the mouth in front of everybody. I looked for the guy who'd made the speech but didn't find him till I went inside where they served lunch. He was already sitting at the table where the other guests were, though no one was talking to him. It was quiet too, not like usual when everyone's talking and shoving. Like someone'd farted and everyone was pretending they couldn't smell it.

This guy, I found out later his name was Patrick, he's real slight, not skinny or anything, just slight. And he had sandy hair and eyes which were dark blue. I thought then he was beautiful though sometimes I think all men are beautiful when I know the facts do not bear this out. But I really thought he was, particularly because he was the first real live in-the-flesh gay man I had ever seen. Apart from Jarrod, that is, who told me he wasn't but he is.

I got a place at the next table. Since I wasn't on lunch duty, I could just sit, watching him. No one was talking to him. I desperately wanted to but didn't know how. Wasn't game. Then lunch came. It was roast beef and vegetables. And when Gillespie got up to say Grace, I saw this guy, Patrick, he didn't have any lunch in front of him. Gillespie said Grace and everyone started to eat. Patrick, this guy, he got up and went to one of the cooks who was standing at the door of the kitchen. People were talking but out of the corner of their eyes, they were beginning to watch. The cook came out and she was looking real uncomfortable when she handed him his tray.

He looks at it, goes all red and just stands there. But then he comes back to where he was sitting and on his tray there's something wrapped up in a brown paper bag. He sits down, opens the bag and takes out a bread roll. Even I can see it's dry and old and the people at his table are embarrassed, except the guy in charge who's carrying on like nothing's happening. But now everyone's looking at this guy and no one's saying a word and I know for sure, this is deliberate. They're punishing Patrick for what he said. They've given him a scungy old bread roll instead of roast beef. Can you believe that?

Patrick, he starts to break the bread roll into pieces and he eats a bit, like it's the most natural thing in the world. And he takes a sip from a glass of water. Everyone's looking at him.

I don't know how it happened. I'm no hero but there's this voice, well not a voice exactly, but something inside me, 'Fuckingwell don't move, you dickwit, don't get involved, they'll kill you.' But that doesn't work. I can't watch him eat that roll all by himself. So suddenly, before I know it, I'm taking the empty seat opposite him. I'm shaking in my boots and my voice doesn't work when I open my mouth. Just a squeak, must have sounded pathetic. And I ask him if I could have a piece of his bread roll too. He smiles, real calm, and his blue eyes are sort of trusting. He offers me a piece of bread and I take it and eat it. It was dry and mouldy but it didn't taste like that. It was so weird, it was fresh. I suppose it was my imagination but that's how it seemed. He offered me half the roll then and I took it.

No one said a word while we were eating. You could hear the currawongs warbling in the trees and the leaves rustling in the breeze. I knew they were going to kill me now but somehow I didn't feel afraid. On the contrary, I was feeling excellent. People started to leave then and that broke the spell and everyone was noisier than usual. I just sat there and Patrick asked me my name and where I lived and what school, that sort of stuff. The priest guy in charge was talking to the guests and saying, so-and-so will take you to the train or so-and-so will drive you home. He came to Patrick and looked down at him and said, 'And you can swim home for all I care.'

Patrick said nothing, like it didn't matter that a priest could behave like this. He stood up to go and he shook my hand and looked into my eyes and said, 'Thank you, you're a very courageous young man.' I can still feel the touch of his hand, even though my hand's like raw meat.

No one said a word to me on the ferry over that afternoon. Or in the bus on the way back. Gillespie made me sit next to him and Mum was waiting with the car at the school when we got back.

'The weekend must have done something good,' Mum said that night. There was an aura around me, she said. 'Won't last,' said Dad.

That night, I kept thinking of what that guy Patrick had said. And about Jarrod, of course.

Next day I knew I had to be real careful, not say anything, just lie low and maybe it would all go away and they wouldn't kill me. It was quiet all day though I could feel them looking at me all the time, talking about me behind my back which was ominous.

After school, I just had to make it to the station. The two danger areas between school and the station are the park opposite the station which you have to cross and the other's the subways you use to get to the platforms. I strolled through the park like there was nothing wrong, in case they were there and thought I was scared, which I was. My stomach was in knots so tight I could hardly walk properly.

I get out of the park and that just leaves the subways and I decide I'll take the one at the end which isn't as busy because they'll think I'll take the busier one. Doesn't matter that people are there. There's been fights there before. I go inside and thank God, it's empty and I relax. Big mistake. They're waiting round the corner where the steps go up to the platform, Lawson, Trentini,

Dooley, O'Halloran, a couple of others.

And Jarrod.

That really threw me. I just stood there. I knew what was going to happen. Lawson's the leader, he started shouting at me like he was so angry, like I'd called his mother a whore or something. 'Faggot, you fucking faggot, we're gunna kill you, you vermin.' And then it was like slow motion in a film. They're all screaming at me, though not Jarrod. He's backed off like he doesn't want to be there. Lawson punches me in the face a couple of times and the others start punching, pushing. I don't know why but I just stood there taking it. I remember I tried not to fall but they pushed me down and started kicking me. It's still all in slow motion.

While I was lying on the ground and they were kicking me, I could see Jarrod staring at me. And his eyes ... Boy, they were really terrible, like he was trapped. And I thought, 'He knows we did it. He knows I know. I might be dying but at least I'm not bullshitting myself.' That thought really got to me and suddenly I knew I had to fight back and I went more berserk than I'd ever been. Apparently I kicked Lawson so hard in the balls that he's had surgery. I was kicking and yelling and screaming and they ran off, all of them. Then I fell down and only came to in casualty with Mum shrieking and weeping over me and Dad looking pretty grim.

The principal ended up telling Mum and Dad it'd be better if they found me another school so Mum told the cops to go for it which they have. Lawson's dad wants to sue me for kicking his son in the balls. Can you believe that?

At last being bashed's saved me from having to tell Mum and Dad I'm gay. Everyone round here must know by now. Mind you, I'm not sure they've really taken it in yet. 'We'll talk about it when you're better,' said Dad.

I just asked Mum to tell Jarrod to come inside if he wants to. Mum said she didn't want him upsetting me but it's even worse, him out there in the cold looking all sad and staring in at me like that. I can hardly sit still as it is. Like I said, I'm nearly jumping out of my skin and him smiling at me, that's always made me sort of melt. Besides, we gotta talk, him and me. Nothing to lose now. You with me, God?

Dear Mum and Dad

Helen Pausacker

Sunday 22nd October

Dear Mum and Dad,

Just before I headed off to catch the train
this afternoon, you said I'd been quieter
than usual and then you asked if everything
was all right. I said, 'Sure, fine,'—and
I've been kicking myself ever since. Because
what I should've said was, 'You've guessed,
haven't you?'

That's right. I'm in love! Kim and I have
been together for over six months now and I
can still hardly believe my luck. I never
dreamed it would be like this, sharing
everything, feeling so incredibly close to
someone.

The first time you met Kim, I was dying
to know what you thought of her. When you
raved about how polite she was and how I'd
found a really nice flatmate, it was a big
relief! Although I felt a bit guilty as
well, because you didn't actually know
that she was your new daughter-in-law.
(Sort of.)

I've been going to this lesbian group at
uni and we've had a few discussions about
coming out to your parents. Some of the
girls said they couldn't be bothered telling

their mum and dad, because they didn't get on with them anyway.

I'm glad our family's not like that. We've always been close—I've never had any secrets from you and the boys. So I feel as though I should've told you about my relationship with Kim before. I'm still not quite sure why I haven't.

Oh well, at least I've told you now. And I'm looking forward to seeing you next weekend and saying all the things I've been wanting to say for months.

Much love, hugs and kisses,

Sue

Monday 23rd October

Dear Mum and Dad,

This is a hard letter to write but I want to be honest with you.

As you know, I've been sharing a flat with Kim Nio for six months now. However, we are not just flatmates but lovers. I am very happy and it's a very solid relationship.

I hope this won't come as a shock to you. I'm still the same Sue that you've always known. As you're both aware, I never had a boyfriend while I was at school. So you may have guessed I was a lesbian anyway.

I'm enclosing a leaflet, 'What every parent should know about homosexuality', for you to read. It has the number of the

Parents of Lesbians and Gays group on it,
if you feel like you need to talk to
someone.

But I'll be coming home at the weekend and
we can discuss it then.

Much love,

Sue

Tuesday 24th October

Dear Mum and Dad,

I just watched the final episode of 'Oranges
are not the Only Fruit' on TV. Did you see
it? ~~I thought of you during the programme~~. I
know you mostly watch the ABC. ~~It's good
that programmes like that~~ Kim and I didn't
miss an episode. We

Wednesday 25th October

Dear Mum and Dad,

Great weather, hey? It's a pity I had to be
stuck indoors, writing my last History essay
for the year. But I've finished it now—five
days before the deadline, which is pretty
good going.

It's been terrific, living here in the
flat. Kim Nio and I get on so well—we never
have arguments over washing dishes or who'll
put the garbage out. We're both studying

really hard but we cook a meal together every night and eat it out on the balcony.

I'm looking forward to seeing you this weekend. Now that I've finished all my essays, we can sit down together and have a good, long rave.

Love,

Sue

Thu 26 Oct

Dear Mum and Dad,

Sorry I won't be able to come home this weekend after all. I'm flat out trying to finish an essay for History which is due on Monday. Hopefully I'll be able to make it next weekend. Love to you, Tom and Brendan,

Sue

POSTCARD

S & B Anderson
25 Caghill Road
Mitcham 3132

The Truth About Love

Ben Widdicombe

I was sitting next to a Swiss before dinner. He had an Italian name and slender, oak-coloured arms. We were talking about love.

'I have been in love several times,' he said.

From the kitchen there was the sound of a ladle hitting the floor and James said, 'Damn.' One of the guests went in to help but was sent out again, quickly.

'Then I think we can't have the same definition of the word.'

It was warm for autumn and the wine had made me drowsy. Luka had been in Oxford a month and was not so quick to drink as me. He was twenty-one, a history student.

'I don't understand,' he said.

'If you've already been in love several times at your age—which is to say, our age—then I don't think we can have the same definition of the word.'

He had a strange way of considering things, Luka, as if he was hearing everything for the first time. I was trying to impress him.

'Well,' he said, 'I love my parents.'

'Exactly. That isn't the sort of love I'm talking about.'

The drawing room was decorated in a deep red wallpaper, post-war and optimistic. Years of damp had spread weird, continental patterns beneath its surface and the worst spots were covered over with photographs and prints.

It was a comfortable room, although I was aware that the man to my left was eavesdropping on our conversation.

'English is a poor language in which to talk about love,' he said. 'The Greeks had five words for it.'

Luka was sitting to my right. He leaned forward on the couch and smiled.

'Did they?' he said. I was annoyed at the interruption.

'And look what happened to them,' I said.

James came to the door and said, 'Soup in five minutes. Is anyone not having soup?'

'What sort of soup is it?' asked a woman with big teeth who was sitting by the window.

'Carrot and coriander,' he said, wiping his hands on a cloth.

'Oh, yes please,' she said and laughed.

'Anyone *not* having?'

Among the six of us in the room there was silence.

'Right then,' he said, and went back into the kitchen.

'What I was talking about,' I said, recapturing Luka's eye, 'is Eros.'

'Ah. The cupid!' The man was leaning further forward now, jamming himself into the conversation like a salesman.

I turned to look at him and for the first time I saw the silver cross on his lapel. He noticed me looking.

'But, I'm being very rude,' he said. 'My name's Francis.'

Francis extended his hand and showed some teeth.

'Duncan,' I said.

'Luka.'

'Cupid has always been the trouble-maker. Right through history.'

'Are you,' I said, 'connected with the university?'

Francis sat slightly back in his seat, an unexpected payoff. 'In a way,' he said, and then '... but not any more, not really. And you?'

'I'm at Pembroke,' I said.

'And your friend?'

'Yes,' said Luka, 'I'm new. I've come to read History.'

'And are you one of James's, er, *flock*?'

He put stress on that last word, and his cross glinted with irony.

'He's my tutor, if that's what you mean.'

'James is frightfully clever, you know. When he was your age he knew Auden at Cambridge ...'

I set my empty glass on the table, breaking their rapport with its chime.

'Do you suppose there's any more wine? Would you like some more wine?'

'I'm okay,' said Luka.

'I think there's some in the kitchen,' said Francis.

'Right then. I'll be right back.' I stood up quickly, hoping Francis would take the hint to butt out when I returned.

Threading my way through the knees and the tea cups, I found the kitchen, where James was stirring a large saucepan on the stove. The table was laid for seven and the room was pleasantly warm.

'How are you doing?' I said.

James turned around and smiled. 'Not so bad,' he said. 'God knows I haven't done this in years.'

On the shelf where the spices should have been was a photograph of James and Kit, middle-aged and together, sitting on a child's slide in a park. It was taken on a winter's day and their cheeks were puffed and rosy.

'Kit always did the lunches,' he said and his voice trailed off.

'Who's Francis?' I said, trying to change the subject. 'I haven't met him before.'

'No, you wouldn't have. He was a friend of Kit's, actually. Well, I say a friend ...'

'Did he meet him doing counselling?'

'Francis was sent. It was a condition of his suspended sentence.'

'*No!* Cottaging?'

'Francis got into loads of trouble. He would pick a gents loo by the police station, wouldn't he?'

'And Kit had to deal with him?'

'He used to go in every Saturday. You're not supposed to have your clients round socially, but you know what Kit was like.'

'Yes, he would bring him home. Francis does have something of the lost dog about him.'

'Mmm ...' said James, losing himself in the swirling soup. Kit's rings bounced on a chain around his neck. After a moment he said, 'Right, you, out of the kitchen. First course in three minutes.'

Taking the cue to be jolly, I bustled to the fridge and took out a fresh bottle of wine. 'Just gettin' some more booze, guv.'

'You'll drink me out of house and home, you will,' he said and I did a little skip over the threshold, back into the drawing-room.

While I was gone, Francis had moved closer to Luka on the couch. I plonked myself between them.

'That's better,' I said.

'Luka was just telling me that he's been in love no

fewer than three times,' said Francis. He seemed proud to have got the information before me.

'Three?' I said. 'That's interesting.'

'But surely you must have been in love too,' said Francis.

I poured myself some more wine.

'I have been ... devoted to people, yes. Infatuated. But never in love.'

'What's the difference?'

'Well, I've been made *unhappy* by a lover, yes. But I've never been made happy.'

Something shifted beneath Luka's eyes. Understanding, perhaps.

'Love should be about happiness,' he said. 'It should be *the* happiness.'

'Love is about loneliness,' I said. 'And loss.'

I thought for a moment of James and Kit on their slide, red-cheeked and happy. I wondered whether the photograph had been taken in the winter just gone, when Kit came home from the hospital.

'But loss,' said Luka, 'loss is a consequence of having had something.'

'Of ownership, you mean.'

'No, not ownership. Well, ownership if you like. I don't know the word in English.'

'You speak very fine English,' said Francis, re-inserting himself into the conversation. Luka smiled.

'Thank you,' he said. 'But what do you think?'

'About love?'

'Yes. About love.'

Francis indulged himself in a long pause. I used the moment to examine Luka's collar bones, which were delicate and well defined and seemed used to being inside expensive shirts.

Francis spoke.

'Some say, you know, that the only truly fulfilling love can be between man and God.'

'I'm not sure I can comment on that,' I said.

'Oh, but you must.' He smiled that ingratiating, parish-priest smile. 'Every man must.'

'My mother used to tell me that there could be no love outside the sight of God,' said Luka. 'But then, I was brought up Catholic.'

Francis smiled at him as if such things could be overcome. 'Love is God's most perfect creation. God is love.'

I had no intention of letting my conversation be hijacked by Francis and his Bible, even if it was Sunday. He was middle-aged and used, and he had no right impinging on my inquiry into love. Or Luka.

'But not all love takes place in the sight of God. Isn't that the case, Francis?'

I had been drinking or I wouldn't have said it.

Francis made a steeple with his fingers.

'What makes you say that?'

Someone addressed the woman with the big teeth as Marigold. They said, 'Marigold, come here' and she did. I followed her across the room with my eyes, trying to think of an answer.

In the end, Francis helped.

'God is the font of all love,' he said, 'for He is its Creator.'

'But not all love is sanctioned by God, is it?'

'I don't know what you mean.'

'Not all love has His approval.'

'Such as?'

Luka was sitting upright in his seat, alert to every word. I began to tread carefully.

'Love of money, for example. That's not sanctioned.'

Francis laughed a treacherous, teacherly sort of laugh. 'Duncan, you're having a joke with us. That's not love, that's a sin. That's avarice.'

'As is ... coveting your neighbour's wife?'

'Most certainly. That's a sin also.'

'But can you not love your neighbour's wife?'

'Perhaps. But you're not supposed to.'

'But you can.'

'Yes.'

'Then did God create that love or not?'

'I suppose so. But he created temptation to be resisted.'

'Ah, but surely that's contradictory ...'

Francis took my hand.

'Duncan,' he said and squeezed, 'there is a place for all love in God's sight. Sometimes, that's all you need to know.'

I remember the look in his eyes when he said it, hollow and hopeful and lonely all at once. I thought of him being caught in that cold lavatory and at that moment I was ashamed of how I'd treated him.

'Soup is served,' James said from the kitchen door and banged a little hand-gong. Francis let go of my hand.

'I see,' I said.

Marigold came over and tugged him on the sleeve.

'Come on,' she said, 'we don't want to miss it.'

'Husbands and wives can't sit together, that's the rule,' said James, turning back into the kitchen.

'Of course we can,' said Marigold and hoisted Francis up from the couch. She turned to Luka and me and added in a stage-whisper, 'We're newly-weds, you know.'

I looked at Francis, then Marigold, and then back to Francis.

'It's true,' he said, as she marched him towards the

kitchen. At the door he turned to us and smiled.

The others followed but I fussed for a moment with some crumbs on my lap until Luka and I were the only ones left in the room. He was swilling the last of the wine around in his glass, watching the patterns it made in the bowl.

'What you said about love,' he said, 'it's sad.'

'You mean about God?'

'No. About loneliness.'

I was suddenly embarrassed; speechless. Luka saw my awkwardness and got up from his seat.

'Come on,' he said, and stretched out his hand. 'Perhaps we'll fall in love over the soup.'

Playing with Fire

Jenny Pausacker

The TV was always on in the lounge room. The curtains were drawn early and the walls flickered with reflected light. Soaps and game shows and sitcoms. Her father planting himself in the middle of the couch to watch the news. Her sister, feet hooked over the back of a chair like bat's claws, watching 'The Simpsons' upside down. Dinner in front of 'Australia's Funniest Home Video Show' and then sport or a movie or one of her mother's travel shows—or all of them at once, if her brother got hold of the remote and went channelsurfing. Sometimes, when he didn't have a job interview next day, he watched NBC and rock clips and old cop shows until dawn. So, as far as she was concerned, the TV was always on.

Not that she cared. In fact, she hardly even noticed, because she usually went straight to her room to redraft an essay or draw up her latest countdown-to-the-end-of-the-year study plan. She had to work hard. She wasn't a natural, not like Trudi who could prop her elbow on a pile of books and argue about whether Silicon Fish was a better band than Serial Killers and then get up and walk away, knowing what was in every one of the books. Life was nice and easy for some people, right? but she'd need to spend every spare moment studying, if she wanted to get the kind of marks that would take her off to law school with Trudi.

All of which made TV watching a definite waste of time.

Except every now and then, like the night when the words started to melt and run together and drip off the page in front of her. She stood up, rubbed her eyes and went to find a snack. The lounge room was empty but the TV was on: two women chatting together, one with a strong lined face and iron grey hair divided by a lightning flash of white, the other young and rosy with round interested eyes. Something about them snagged her attention and she paused in the middle of the room to listen. Went to perch on the arm of the couch. Slid down and slumped against a stack of cushions.

It was an English cop show, more Agatha Christie than gritty realism. The two women—Inspector Fox and Sergeant Fletcher—seemed to be investigating a murder with overtones of witchcraft and for a while she entertained herself by trying to guess the murderer and fill in the scenes that she'd missed. But then strange things started happening—a dead black cat on Fox's doorstep, words scrawled on the wall in a room that no one could've entered. The rosy sergeant stayed sceptical but the inspector's grey eyes became progressively more shadowed until, nerves on edge, suspicious of everyone around her, she bolted from the police commissioner's office, crying out, 'Where's Fletcher? *I want Fletcher.*'

I want Fletcher. The words flared, bright and dangerous as a lighted match flicked at her from the opposite side of the lounge room. (Hadn't Trudi said that the woman who played Fox had made her name acting in Shakespeare?) She found herself sitting bolt upright, watching the screen with aching concentration, waiting for the next meeting between the two women. A few scenes later Fletcher came looking for Fox, Fox glanced up from her desk and smiled wryly—and the picture blinked and changed to a row of dancing potato chips. She turned to see her brother on the couch beside her, levelling the remote like a handgun.

'Put it down,' she ordered. 'Can't you see I'm watching this?' and he dropped the remote and backed away, leaving her on her own again.

For the space of two heartbeats she felt guilty. Then she forgot and leaned forward and watched Fox and Fletcher, tracking clues, questioning suspects, discovering that the police commissioner was the head of a coven. Finally the logic of the plot brought her to the moment when the two women faced each other and exchanged a look of satisfied understanding. She glanced sideways, to make sure she was still alone in the lounge room, and then she sighed.

When she stood up, her midriff felt bruised and tender, as if the organs it protected were growing and changing underneath its pad of flesh. She made a sandwich in the kitchen and carried it back to her room but she couldn't eat, because her stomach was churning.

'Where's Fletcher?' she whispered experimentally. Her throat clenched tight before she could practise saying, '*I want Fletcher.*'

I lay awake for hours. My heart thumping so hard that I got high on all the oxygen in my bloodstream. I kept seeing those two women's faces. Kept hearing those words. Kept trying to remember more about 'Fox and Fletcher'. I'd watched the first episode and bits of a few others but they hadn't struck me as anything special: not like now.

Next morning I woke out of a deep stunned sleep and remembered something. Raced to school, grabbed Trudi, hissed, 'Listen, you're a "Fox and Fletcher" fan, aren't you? Any chance that you taped it last night?'

She nodded. 'Yeah, sure. I was at my Tae Kwon Do class, so I set the VCR and watched it when I got home.'

'Good,' I said. 'Because I missed the end of it. Can I swap with you, Trude? A clean tape in return for "Fox and Fletcher"?'

She nodded again, so I went back to her house that afternoon. Didn't matter how hard I was studying, I could always make time to see Trudi. I'd just go home afterwards and rearrange my study plans all over again.

We raved on for a while, as usual, and then she went to get the tape out of the VCR. Ever noticed how oil refineries have those tall silver pipes with a flame on top that burns off the waste gases and flares up more brightly whenever there's more waste? Well, when Trudi dropped the tape into my hand, it felt as though something released inside me and sent a jet of flame searing up my spine. My brain blazed. Every cell in my body was on fire with excitement.

'Thanks,' I said from a tight throat. 'I'll do the same for you some day.'

She'd always been the reliable one in her family. Her sister was trouble in black leggings, her brother was unemployed and unhappy, so somebody had to take the middle ground. But she started by lying to Trudi—she *hadn't* missed the end of 'Fox and Fletcher'—and before long she seemed to be sneaking and scheming all the time.

Because suddenly there were a lot of things she needed to do. She had to tape the rest of the 'Fox and Fletcher' series. She had to rummage through the pile of old newspapers in the laundry and make a list of the episodes she'd missed. She had to find time to watch the witchcraft episode again (and again and again). And she had to do all this in secret, without her family noticing. Not easy, considering the amount of time they spent in front of the TV.

She stuck to her study plans but now her life was planned around 'Fox and Fletcher' as well. She was desolate when the series ended. Ecstatic when the station started to repeat it. Chair-kicking furious when she sat down to watch the sixth episode and found that it had been shunted aside by a telecast of some footie match. Next week, to her relief, the show was back again but a fortnight later a programmer checked its ratings, drew a line through it and replaced it with 'McGyver'.

Instant outrage, followed by a week of feeling bereft and powerless. Still, at least she's got her checklist. There are twenty episodes of 'Fox and Fletcher' in total and she's taped fifteen of them. Only five to go. She wants them. She's never felt more determined in her life.

She tries all the video shops in her area, phones retail outlets and specialist shops and finally gets the name of a mail order service in Manchester. An exchange of air-letters, a bank draft—there go her savings—and then she settles down to wait for a parcel from England. And in the meantime she watches her fifteen tapes again (and again and again).

Over time a pattern of moments starts to develop. There's the episode where Fletcher leans past Fox to click the mouse on the computer and their hands almost touch. The episode where Fox teases Fletcher, as usual, and Fletcher, unusually, shows that she's hurt. And, of course, the episode where Fox gasps, 'I want Fletcher.' Soon she knows all those moments so well that she can replay them in her mind whenever she likes: no need for a VCR. Soon she starts to extend them and turn them into a story of her own.

It's hard to say exactly when the story turns into a romance.

Fox is sulking because Fletcher understands the computer better than she does. She looks so distinguished, lined face and dark grey hair, but she can be quite childish at times. She won't move over and let Fletcher open the relevant files, so Fletcher has to keep reaching across her. Then they both go for the mouse at the same time and Fletcher's hand closes over Fox's hand (yes!) and Fox glances up with that quizzical lift of her eyebrows— Fletcher's staring at her, breathing fast—a hopeful look in her round eyes but it doesn't take her long to realise that Fox isn't feeling the same way. She sighs and—

Wait a minute. Too obvious. Inspector Fox is the brilliant moody one: Sergeant Fletcher's job is to be calm and ordinary and stabilise things. Besides, if Fletcher reacts too much now, it spoils the next part. So, okay, she feels all this stuff but she doesn't let it show. Then later on Fox makes some sarcastic comment like, 'We almost missed a vital clue while we were holding hands in front of the computer.' (Not quite right—need to work on that.) Anyhow, this time Fletcher actually ... flinches? mouth quivers? tears in her eyes? (Nah, she's not that much of a wimp.) Fletcher stares at Fox, steady and confronting, her rosy cheeks slightly redder than usual. Fox shrugs—she never takes much notice of other people's weak spots—and makes another crack. So Fletcher walks out.

Cut to Fox alone in the office, standing by the window. You can tell she's feeling a bit bad about the way she treated Fletcher but she doesn't have time to think it through, because just then the police commissioner knocks on her door. Fast forward through some boring plot business to the point where Fox starts to get really upset. The point where she storms off, going, 'Where's Fletcher? I want Fletcher.'

And—oh Jesus, *of course*—Fletcher's there. (Should've realised that before.) She came back and she's standing at the end of the corridor and she hears Fox and walks towards her and takes her in her arms and—hey, hold on. Way too fast. It wouldn't happen like that, not after so many years where Fox went on falling for all those impossible men and Fletcher kept her feelings under wraps. Still, there's something in it, just the same.

All right. Play it again.

The teachers kept telling us that our final year of school would be the most difficult ever but what can I say? it wasn't like that for me. I worked hard and fast, in order to get back to Fox and Fletcher. Told their story to myself in the shower, on my way to school, during study breaks, at night before I went to sleep. The joy of figuring out a new development. The steady satisfaction of replaying the existing scenes. Words and ideas came spooling out of me even more freely than I imagined they would when I became a barrister, making speeches to a crowded courtroom. (Or doing whatever lawyers do. I was starting to get the feeling that law mightn't be quite as glamorous as it looked on TV.)

It changed me. I hadn't realised how much I did for my family until I stopped. My brother used to get me to write his job applications. My sister used to lie on my bed and tell me how unfair everything was. My mother and father used to corner me in the kitchen and worry about my brother and sister. But not any more. I wasn't cooperating these days. Didn't have time.

Fox and Fletcher even changed things with Trudi. She was an 'F&F' fan too, remember, so I couldn't help wondering. Dropped a few hints— 'Y'know, if one of those two was a guy, you'd assume they fancied each other'— but she just laughed and I didn't have the nerve to push it. I realised then that although Trudi and I talked serious, we didn't talk personal. The first time I'd ever thought she was less than perfect.

Still, it wasn't a problem. Nothing was, then. I'd never been so happy, my life had never been so intense. Up until that night in front of the TV, I hadn't really been able to understand why people bothered about love but all of a sudden I was going around silently apologising to every kid who'd ever raved on to me about guys or pop stars. I could see through their eyes now. Could see that magic aura, because it glowed around Fox and Fletcher, transforming their slightest change of expression, making their unspectacular faces beautiful.

Funny, though: I wasn't actually in love with Fox, or with Fletcher. I don't know whether this makes sense but I seemed to be in love with both of them at once.

Months pass. Life goes on. Her brother gets a job in a pub for five weeks, her sister is sent home for swearing at the sports teacher, her mother announces that she's going to Tasmania with her Tattslotto syndicate, her father scores a load of free wood from his cousin and pulls a muscle chopping it. And in her stories the two women have taken to sitting side by side, Fletcher's arm stretched out across the back of the couch. Finally

Fletcher shifts slightly. Fox turns, into her embrace.
They kiss. They—

What?

She's not sure.

For the first half dozen replays she just sends them off
into the bedroom, cuts straight to the next morning. But
before long her ignorance starts to get irritating. It's her
story, after all. She wants to know.

Determination can't help her this time. Her fifteen
'Fox and Fletcher' tapes don't help either. The story is
stalled for several weeks until, one morning when she's
flicking through the paper, she catches a brief mention
of a local gay bookshop. She hunts for its address in the
phone book. Goes there. Walks up and down the street,
up and down. She's terrified—far too terrified to work
out what's frightening her. Then she thinks, 'I don't
have to do this. I could just go home', and that thought
sends her striding into the shop.

The shelves are the same, the rows of spines are
the same as in any other bookshop. Her heart kicks once
at the sight of a sign saying LESBIAN FICTION and
then she settles down to browse along the shelves.
There's a novel about cowgirls on a ranch in America, a
novel called *Sappho's Daughter* set in Ancient Greece.
And a novel about two women who meet and go to bed
together, quarrel and go to bed together, separate and
miss going to bed together, make up and go to bed
together.

When she finally looks up from the pages, she's surprised to find she's still in the bookshop. Who would've
guessed there were so many different ways of having sex?
She tucks the book under her arm but she has to roam
around for ten minutes before she can go and pay for it.
Impossible to look the woman behind the counter in the

eye, while her nipples are standing like beacons and a pulse of nerve endings keeps rippling in her groin.

Back home she hides the book in a suitcase on top of her cupboard, along with the 'Fox and Fletcher' tapes. (Her sister won't find it there.) She reads it late at night, half-hidden behind her second pillow, with another book close at hand so that she can snatch it up if her mother comes in. The book itself isn't all that compelling but when she applies her new information to Fox and Fletcher, it takes her breath away. A whole extra dimension. She's always been in love with Fox and Fletcher but now they're just as urgently in love with each other.

She's lying in bed one night, rehearsing her story, when it occurs to her that Trudi is like the charismatic inspector, she is like the loyal sergeant. Some alarming implications here but she refuses to be alarmed. Instead she treats the idea as if it was one of her assignments. Tests it with logical analysis and concludes that, even though she feels like Fletcher around Trudi, in some ways she's probably more like Fox. (Moody. Defensive. Talking big to hide her feelings. Just like Fox.) So it's more complicated than it looks at first. Although it could explain why she's in love with both Fox and Fletcher.

Weeks pass. She's in bed with her book, reading it for the twentieth time, when she notices that half the things the two characters do together are things you could easily do on your own. So she turns out the light. She grips one nipple cautiously between thumb and fore-finger, squeezes it, rolls it, pulls it. While her other hand burrows through crisp curls to find some mysterious pleats of flesh which she prods methodically until she feels a responsive twinge. She leans back, hands keeping the rhythm, eyebrows pulled together in a puzzled frown: not half as excited as when she's replaying a scene from her story. And then there's a sound in her ears like a high wind. Shock waves jolt outwards from her fingertips and her hips bounce off the mattress. In that electric instant she tries to push herself into the story that she's been telling.

But she doesn't gasp 'Fox' or 'Fletcher'.

She gasps, 'Trudi!'

—Prisoner at the bar, you stand accused of wasting your time on B-grade fantasies that promote unhealthy attitudes and pose a serious threat to your chance of a normal life. How do you plead: guilty or not guilty?

—Guilty. No, not guilty. Oh hell, I don't know.

—Very well then, we shall proceed straight to the cross-examination. Do you or do you not spend at least ten hours of every week inventing a homosexual fantasy in which the main characters are thinly disguised versions of yourself and one of your classmates?

—No way. You've got it all wrong. Fox and Fletcher are *real*.

—Real? Pardon me if I find that a little difficult to accept.

—You don't have to be sarcastic about it. Okay, I know Fox and Fletcher aren't real like my family or the kids at school. But they come from a real series on TV. They're real to me.

—I see. So your defence is that these regrettable fantasies have, as it were, a life of their own. Nonetheless, wouldn't it be true to say that, on the night of July the twenty-third, you identified one of the principal characters as being based on Trudi Louise Cartwright, your best friend for the past five years?

—Look, maybe that's part of it. But so what? I mean, I'm not in love with Trudi or anything. I'd know.

—Would you? Can you look me in the eye and solemnly swear that you have never, on any other date, implicated Trudi Louise Cartwright in your pornographic imaginings?

—All right, there was the time when I was, um, touching myself—but that was an accident. And once or twice since then I've accidentally thought about kissing her. Nothing more than that, though. I couldn't. It'd be *embarrassing*.

—Embarrassing, eh? Merely embarrassing, not childish or shameful or wilfully self-destructive? Tell me, prisoner at the bar, would I be right in assuming that you spend more time on your fantasies than you spend with your family and friends?

— ... Yes.

—And are you asking the court to believe that you regard this as a positive development?

—Yes! Fact is, I was miserable before I lucked onto Fox and Fletcher. They changed things for me. They changed everything.

—Indeed? Could you be so kind as to explain that last statement to the court?

—Um. Not really. No. I can't explain. And it worries me too, sometimes.

—Aha! I'm glad to hear that you have some vestiges of proper feeling. So you admit that you're troubled by this unfortunate obsession?

—Yes, but—

—That is the case for the prosecution. Prisoner at the bar, I advise you to enter a plea of guilty, although I warn you I shall recommend that you be sentenced to give up your fantasies forever.

—Sorry, not a chance. I couldn't give up Fox and Fletcher, no matter what you say. They're the only thing that makes me happy.

Three months after I'd posted off the bank draft, my five 'Fox and Fletcher' tapes arrived. (Couldn't afford airmail postage and apparently seamail takes forever.) Mum noticed the stamps and asked a few questions but I told her I'd sent away for some special English history books, which seemed to satisfy her. I took the parcel into my room. Tore off the wrapping. Sat on the bed for ages, touching the cover photos of Fox and Fletcher and wondering how I was going to manage ten private hours in front of the TV.

Sometimes life is kind. That weekend one of my brother's friends asked him down to his family's beach house. So on Friday night I raced through my assignments and my revision, checked to make sure that my mother and father had gone to bed and crept into the lounge room. It was dark for once, only a red glow from the last of the fire. Shadows shrouded the TV and piled up in the corners, so high they looked as though they might collapse and topple onto me. By the time I found the lamp beside the couch, my heart was beating like a drum.

I was standing next to the TV with one of the new tapes in my hand when my sister walked in. She should've been in bed. I would've been, at her age. But she thought she could do whatever she liked and she was right, too. Mum and Dad never came down on her the way they did on me, because they were scared she'd chuck a whammy. She got away with murder. I hated her.

'Don't look at me like that,' she whinged. 'It isn't fair.

You're never around these days and I've been wanting to ask you something.'

'Well, you can't, I said. 'Not now. You ought to be asleep.'

'Yeah, right. How am I supposed to sleep when my best friend's mad at me and my sister won't even talk to me about it?'

'You could try sorting out your own problems, like everybody else has to. Face it, I don't have time for that sort of thing at present. I'm too busy studying, in case you hadn't noticed.'

'You're not studying now.'

'Oh wow, that's so perceptive. No, I'm not studying—I'm taking a break for once and I want to spend it relaxing, not listening to you bitch about Annamaria Borlotti. Now, are you going to piss off so I can watch my video in peace?'

My sister scowled. She said, 'Fuck your video.' Grabbed it from me and threw it onto the fire.

Slow motion, the slowest ever. The tape, cartwheeling through the air. Dropping down. One corner strikes the raft of burning coals and it splits apart, releasing a sail of orange flame. Soft. Tissue-thin. The colour of sunset.

I'd been over near the TV but now, miraculously, I'm kneeling in front of the fireplace. I reach through the flame. Towards the video. I save it. Bubbling plastic, a sick smell and a blister where Fletcher's face used to be but I wrench the cover open and tip out the sleek black unblemished case of the video cassette.

Then I look down at my hand.

'Oh shit,' my sister says in awe. 'You're even crazier than me.'

They're in the bathroom with the door shut. Automatic conspirators: no point letting the parents in on this. Her sister removes the ice pack, smooths white cream across scarlet skin.

'Okay, what's the big deal? It's just a 'Fox and Fletcher' tape. Why was it so fucking important?'

'Because.' How do you say something to a member of your own family that you've never said to anybody else? 'You wouldn't understand.'

'Try me.'

'Well, because it's special?'

'How come?'

'Because I can see something in it that no one else can see.'

'Like what?'

'The two women. They're ... close.'

'Lesos, you mean?'

'That's what I think.'

'So? What's special about that?'

'Well, I'm a lesbian too.'

It's not just that she's never said it before: she's never even fully thought it. But her sister doesn't seem all that surprised.

'Hey, cool. That ought to shake things up around here. I reckon you should get your hair cut like k.d. lang. You're doing it with Trudi, right?'

'No. I couldn't. Trudi's not—'

'How do you know?'

Silence in the bathroom. Her sister winds gauze tape around her fingers and fastens it at the wrist. 'I learnt this in Health and Human Relations,' she comments. 'About the only useful thing they've ever taught me at school. How does it feel?'

'Better. Still throbbing, though ... Listen, do you want to talk about Annamaria now?'

'Jesus, you *are* a weirdo! You'd have to be joking. I wouldn't dump my stuff on you after—after that. I'm going to bed, and so should you.'

'All right. Just one more thing before you go. What the hell am I supposed to say to Mum in the morning?'

'Easy. Tell her you spilled boiling water when you were making coffee, of course.' Her sister pats her on the shoulder and looks at her with friendly contempt. 'You don't know the first thing about lying, do you? Never mind. You'll learn.'

I went back into the lounge room to switch off the lamp. Fire in my hand but a gentle warmth in my midriff. I'd talked to someone in my family about something that mattered to me. A first. Another thing I owed to Fox and Fletcher.

I reached for the lamp with my right hand but the skin on my fingers stretched so tight that they couldn't move. So I left the lamp on. Went back to my room and took down the suitcase, one-handed. A brotherless weekend, which meant I could watch videos till dawn if I liked. No one would notice. In our lounge room the TV was always on.

I sat cross-legged on the floor near the TV, arranging my twenty tapes in chronological order. Cradled my hand, smiled at the blistered cover. But picked up one of the old tapes first and went fast forward straight to the right spot.

'Where's Fletcher?' Fox asked urgently.

My hand burned in my lap and my lips moved in time with hers as she cried out, '*I want Fletcher.*'

Silence

Lucy Sussex

1. The badge

Silence isn't golden. I think it must be a dull grey, with flashes of red here and there, for anger. Not bright and shiny, nothing like the gilded badge Mikal wore on his leather jacket. We put it *there*—see?—centre left.

It looks gold but it's really glazed clay: Ma's work. One of the few times my parents collaborated, apart from on me, as Dad says, was the big clay sculpture they made when they got sick of trying to explain the complex ins and outs of the family tree, all the steps and halfs and odds. They exhibited the clay tree but nobody bought it, 'Because it looked like somebody else's Christmas,' Ma said sadly. But that gave her an idea and next Christmas she took each little clay emblem off the tree and gave them to the family member they represented. Dad had the mallet, Ma the little potter's wheel. The tree itself ended up as our hatstand.

It's the spring after that Christmas and I'm climbing the big cherry tree in blossom, something even Ma and Dad forbid, when I look down to see a *strange man* gazing up at me. I suddenly remember last night's TV news, and the lead item: a kid my age abducted while riding her little blue bike.

The thought makes me lose my footing and down I fall, into leather-jacketed arms. I tense, about to scream the house and garden down, then recognise the M pinned to his lapel. It's the twin of the Z on

my jumper, except that mine has a silvery glaze, his gold-
en. M for ...

'You have to be Mikal,' I say, with as much dignity as
you can manage, when you're lying on your back in a
total stranger's arms.

'And you're my famous niece Zilla,' he says in one of
those funny English accents, as he sets me on my feet. I
look up at him. He's a bit like Dad, but his hair is brown,
not grizzled, and there's a lot of it, sticking out like wires
around his head.

'Sweet Jesus!' and that's Dad, running down the garden, covered in stone dust, as usual. 'Do my eyes deceive
me? Mikal?'

'Yeah, I'm back,' Mikal says and suddenly all of us—
Mikal, me, Dad even a clayey Ma—are hugging underneath the cherry blossom.

'How's your mother these days?' asks Dad, after several beers back at the house. His voice is uneasy—even I
know he's nervous of his stepmother.

'Getting married again,' Mikal says.

'Ooh, that's nice,' says Ma. 'Who's the lucky man?'

'God, actually.'

'Sweet Jesus!' That's Dad.

'No,' Mikal says, 'not the Son. The Father. A convent
in Norfolk have accepted my mother as a novice.' The
way he says it, she could have just gone up the road to
the supermarket.

'She always was religious,' Dad says dubiously. Then,
to change the subject: 'Well, how's the painting going?
You must be in your last year at the Academy now, you
lucky devil.'

Mikal pauses, running his fingers through his hair.

'Gave it the flick.'

'Nooo!' That's both parents, much more upset and

surprised than they were about my step-grandma becoming a nun.

'Look, no offense, but I want to do ... something that won't take me twenty years to perfect, even if I could get it perfect. And that might be of benefit to other people.'

He says this very seriously but with a sweet smile. It works. Dad's momentarily rueful, Ma instantly understanding.

'So now I've come back,' he says, 'to meet the likes of Zilla, and start anew.'

We didn't know it then, but that was the beginning of his long goodbye.

2. Spangles

How can I put it? Mikal became part of my family life but at the same time separate from us. He did a one-year course in counselling—somehow we never learnt where, nor whom he was supposed to be counselling. Nor were we ever quite sure of his address. Weeks would pass with Mikal off in his own world, then he would breeze into the house unannounced, merrily disrupt the sculpting or potting or my homework, then breeze out again.

'Stormy petrel,' Ma said to Dad once, after an evening in which they had determined to quiz him but had not quite been able to, because Mikal had as usual disarmed and distracted them completely.

'Yes, but he must lay his head somewhere ...'

'He has his own life to lead,' Ma said.

See the spangles, beside the badge? They weren't sewn by me but by another of Mikal's many friends. Yet I look at them and think of a long-ago afternoon, Mikal playing Barbie doll with me, constructing extraordinary costumes for her out of Christmas tinsel, ribbon, glitter.

'Mardi Gras Barbie!' he says, laughing as the doll gets more and more extreme. Ma comes in to see what the fun is about and at the sight of the doll gives Mikal an odd quick glance. He meets her gaze and she looks away.

I know now how those two made an unspoken pact. Mikal had his privacy, Ma respected that. And so between his evasions and her reticence was laid the foundation of all our silence.

3. The background

Like it? We think it's by Mikal, as far as we can be sure. Ru, Mikal's flatmate, brought us this canvas, which he'd found at the bottom of a trunk, so we could authenticate it. The unspoken question hung in the air: can't we ask Sister Anne, Mikal's mum? But nobody would voice it.

'Mikal an abstract expressionist?' Dad said finally. 'People do change style in art school.'

It looked like an unfinished sketch to me: thin washes of greys, red, and peacock blue, with most of the canvas left creamy bare.

'Can I keep it?' Ru says.

'Of course,' Ma says instantly.

'Could even throw in a frame,' Dad adds.

'Oh, I won't need that,' Ru says and spreading the canvas wide, gets out a tape measure. 'Thought so,' he comments. 'Just the right size.'

'For what?' says Ma.

Ru doesn't answer immediately. Instead he puts his pointy chin in his hands, staring down at the canvas intently.

And Dad says, suddenly: 'No.'

Ru looks up, his glance stabbing. 'Yes!'

They argue until nearly dawn, when a compromise is reached. Ru can do what he wants with the canvas, but no name is to appear on it.

'Not even Mikal?' I protest.

'The spelling's too distinctive,' Dad says wearily.

It's Ma, in the end, who suggests the 'M' of the brooch, her contribution to the Mikal collage.

4. Moggy

I wonder if I'd ever have found out, having been excluded from the Conspiracy of Silence like Sister Anne, if Mikal hadn't been forced to trust me. It was all Moggy's fault. Mikal wanted to show me his new kitten, a scruffy ball of black and white fluff, but very cute. He left us alone while he said a quick hi to Ma over the kiln, and Moggy went and climbed under the flap of his shoulder bag. Of course I had to open it to get him out and he struggled, bringing with him this interesting magazine.

'Oh!' says Mikal, returning just as I disentangle Moggy, the magazine flopping open at a centrefold. He goes bright red in the face. Making the most of the opportunity before he snatches the magazine away, I flip through the pages.

'Like *Playboy*,' I say. 'But no girls.'

'Er, no.'

'You don't like girls?'

'Of course I do. Just not in the *Playboy* way.'

I've scanned all the art books in the house, with their Davids, Adams and other beefcake. But though the men in Mikal's magazine are naked, what they are doing has never been depicted in any artwork I've seen.

'Do you think, Zilla,' he says gently, 'that you could

give the magazine back to me? Because I really find this embarrassing.'

I return the magazine to Mikal, who stows it in his bag. He eyes me. 'So much for the dire effect of pornography on innocent youth! You couldn't care less, could you?'

I shrug. 'There's nothing in it for me.'

'True — but you won't talk about this at school, will you? Or to anyone else?'

Looking up, I see that he is rigid with anxiety.

'If Moggy won't blab, then I won't either.'

We shake on it, and shake Moggy's little paw too. That's all very silly, but what isn't silly is the kiss Mikal gives me as he leaves, the kitten peeping over the zip of his leather jacket. It signals adulthood, respect.

Now I'm standing beside Ru in the flat, looking down at the silkscreened image of a cat's mask.

'Moggy goes on next,' he says, and at the name a huge pillow of black and white fur in the best chair lifts his head sleepily.

'I'm glad!'

'Can't leave out an important part of Mikal's life,' he says, adding in afterthought: 'And mine too.'

'Did Mikal ever tell you,' I say, 'about Moggy and the copy of *Men Only*?'

'Uh-huh. And then you caught him out a second time ...'

I squirm, remembering, and suddenly it's autumn of the previous year and I'm wandering through the city, playing hookey. A man comes out of a doorway in front of me. I recognise brown wiry hair, a leather jacket.

'Mikal!'

'Huh?' and he looks around. For a moment he looks right through me and I see that he's pasty pale and swaying on his feet. I walk up to him and put my arm around his waist. He leans against me, his head on my shoulder, for we are almost the same height now.

'What's up? Flu?'

He shakes his head and at that I see the words above the door. 'Cancer Institute'. It hits like a hammer and for a moment I could sway too, but I will myself to stand still and strong. Mikal lifts his head and I see he is focusing on a taxi, crawling along the kerb.

'Zilla, please help me into that cab!'

I do as he asks but hop in as well. Mikal just manages to give an address to the driver, before slumping back in the seat.

'Bad dose of radiotherapy, eh?' says the driver, not unkindly. 'See it all the time, when you pick up fares from here.'

'Where are you sick?' I whisper to Mikal.

He touches his throat, then his arm drops, as if the effort is too much.

The taxi leaves the city and drives towards the beach suburbs, before stopping before a block of flats: Mikal pays the driver, then walks shakily but unaided to a groundfloor flat. The door opens to reveal a small fox of a man, his red hair bristling.

'You did it! You just had to be the big stoic and head off to radiotherapy all by yourself.'

'Ru, meet Zilla. She saved the day.'

Mikal just makes it to a couch before collapsing. Ru stops scolding, bringing doona, pillow, water to drink.

'So now you know Mr Secretive's secret,' he says to me, still mildly exasperated.

'I didn't want people to worry,' Mikal says weakly. 'Just one course of radiotherapy and I'll be all right.'

I think I see what he means and leap in with both

feet. 'Guess you're right. People are scared of the C-word, just like they are of the A-word ...'

If I could go back in time and edit myself, I'd cut that sentence. But there it is. I'm stuck in a linear progression, time's arrow, with nothing to do but cringe at my mistakes. Of course they don't say anything at my blunder. And later, feeling adult at the confidence, I agree not to tell Ma and Dad, in case they tell Mikal's mum, now a full-fledged Sister.

'She'd only pray for me,' Mikal says.

5. A cluster of ribbons

I don't understand what these symbolise, and so I ask Ru.

'One for every person he counselled. He was very good at his job — perhaps because he knew he was going that way himself.'

A photo on the windowsill catches my eye. Mikal in the centre of a group of people, as thin and grey as he was towards the end.

'He knew ... how long did he know?'

'Since before he came back from London.'

'And to be silent so long!' The thought stops my mouth. 'The strain ...'

'It didn't help,' Ru says, bending over the quilt again.

I think he wants me to go home now, but there's something I have to ask. 'You, are you...?'

'No. He told me, and we played safe as houses.'

And there's nothing I can do after that but ride off on my bike, pondering the secrets that people carry around with them, that I carry too, like a pack on my back.

6. LOVE

That was my contribution, above the M, in blue letters.
Because that was all I could give and it wasn't enough
~~this is where it gets difficult~~
to save Mikal from a second and then a third radiotherapy treatment, he getting thinner and greyer as the
tumour got fatter. The day he arrived at our house wearing a hat, Ma opened the door and saw immediately that
he was seriously ill. He waited until we were all gathered
in the living room, then dramatically doffed his hat.

'My head got too cold,' he says.

Dad, in a gesture that would be cruel were it not
unconscious, rubs his scalp, registering that Mikal now is
the balder of the brothers.

'Oh Mikal,' Ma says, sitting down suddenly. 'Oh
Mikal.'

'I've come to tell you,' Mikal says, staring down into
the depths of his hat, 'that I'm going into hospital
tomorrow. For an all-out assault on ...' and he taps his
throat, X-marking the spot of his diseased lymph gland.

'Have you contacted your mother?' That's Ma, finding
her voice again.

'Sent her a letter. I'm not too proud for prayer now,
and who knows? It might even help.'

He says that with his usual smile and slowly, tremu-
lously, we smile back.

That was the last time we saw him. He had never had
surgery before and nobody knew that Dad's allergic reaction to anaesthetics was genetic, also carried by Mikal.
In his weakened state, it was lethal.

7. Dad's contribution

'You have to realise that this was the best way for him, that he had no chance ...'

In the night, I wake to hear Ru's voice and pad down the corridor to the living room. They are all three seated at the table, empty glasses and a nearly empty bottle of red wine between them. I realise that while I cried myself into a fitful sleep, they merely got drunk. Well, I'm old enough to try their remedy now, so I take the bottle from the table.

'No chance for us to say goodbye,' Ma says. She turns her head as I lift the bottle, then merely shrugs. There's less than a wine glass left in the bottle, but still enough to make my head spin.

'No need for him to say goodbye,' Ru says. 'To go to sleep in hope and never wake up, saved from more morphine, more pain, and in the end despair.'

He reaches out an arm and I cuddle into it. He's smaller than Mikal and smells different, but still is welcome.

'You should try International Directory Assistance again,' Ma says to Dad.

He looks irritated. 'They were certain the first time that St Mary's Convent, Norfolk, is unlisted.'

'An express letter, then,' says Ma.

'Saying what?' I cut in, made bold by alcohol.

'That he died from anaesthetic,' Dad says.

Ru again: 'I saw the letter Mikal sent the Sister. Not a thing in it to upset a religious ... apart from the C-word, of course.'

'No need to mention the A-word,' says Dad abruptly. Ma looks at him and I see assent in her glance. Ru's body slumps slightly against mine and the body language tells me he is near the end of his tether, beyond argument.

'Yes, but Ma, you know that if I've done something, you tend to find out. Mother's intuition, you call it. And then you're cross that I didn't tell you!'

'Zilla, you simply don't understand the stigma attached to the disease. Do you want to be tormented at school, because Mikal ...?' Ma stops and suddenly puts her hand to her mouth and bites it.

'Has been punished by God for his deviance,' finishes Dad, brutally. 'That's what Sister Anne would think and it would be hell for her. And I, though I've never got on with the woman, can't bring myself to tell her.'

Thus a promise of silence was extracted from us. Ru left on his motorbike, Ma and I went to the king-sized bed together and Dad stayed up with another bottle of wine. I understood then that grief was something that he preferred to cope with alone, rather than in company.

So he was initially hostile when Ru wanted to use the canvas as the base for a memorial panel in the AIDS Quilt. Yet when it was nearly completed, he carved a tiny soapstone head, a stylised laughing man, with holes drilled in it for sewing to the cloth. And he brought it out shyly, as if he half expected the gift to be refused.

8. ?

That first express letter went astray. The second reached St Mary's only to bring us the message that Sister Anne had left the convent. They did forward her mail, though, and eventually, several months after Mikal's funeral which I can't write about, not just now

Dad and I pile into the car and set off to the airport. Ma stays behind, putting the spare room in order, which since it is the storage space for all the unsold artwork, is a lot of work. Nobody could decide whether or not Anne should meet Ru, so he too stayed away.

She's not so scary — that's my first thought. I don't know what to expect, but there in the arrival lounge is a little, middle-aged woman in black, the only sign of her being not your usual granny the cross pinned to her coat lapel. She shakes hands with me firmly.

'Your father's eyes!' she says to Dad, after scrutinising me. I don't say anything. She has Mikal's accent, and eyes.

In the car, going down the freeway, Dad for once not speeding, the talk is general, non-specific and sparse. Just out of the city centre, the car shudders to a rattling halt.

'Sweet Jesus,' says Dad. 'Oh, Anne, sorry!'

We get out and, though Dad fiddles under the hood, nothing's doing.

'I'll ring for the R.A.C.V. and wait,' he says. 'Zilla, you'll just have to take Anne home on the tram.'

Anne gives me a quick assertive nod and we go round the corner to the tram stop. It stands on the edge of parkland and at the sight her jetlagged face lightens.

'I've been cooped up in a plane for what feels like a week. Do you think we might stretch our legs a little?'

So we walk across the park, wet grass under my Doc Martens and her sensible black shoes, a riot of daffodils and jonquils in every flowerbed. She walks quickly, taking deep breaths of the perfumed air, not a sign of tiredness about her anywhere now. Before I have really taken note of our direction, her brisk steps have taken us within sight of the Exhibition Building.

'Now this I do recognise,' Anne says. 'Even after twenty years away!'

Suddenly an idea comes from nowhere. I reach out to Anne and she, without hesitation, puts her hand in mine. I am half afraid that since I was last here, over a week ago, a motor or horticultural show will have displaced the Quilt but no, the posters haven't changed. We run across the front lawn, up the marble steps and into the great hall to find little groups of people moving between the rectangles of cloth. Third to the right and down six, I recall, and we soon reach our goal, almost skidding to a halt in front of Mikal's flag.

Anne stands beside me panting, gazing down at all our loving work: the ribbons and spangles, the soapstone carving, Moggy and all the rest. For a moment I think she has not seen Mikal for so long that there may be nothing here she will recognise. But then she kneels, caressing the painted sketch of the background, her fingers moving over LOVE, tracing out each letter, then the clay M. Her face turns to me and I see her expression, peaceful, smiling even, at this tribute to her son.

I know that I can now explain each feature of the collage to her and in the end ask:

'And what will *you* contribute?'

Staying in

Dean Kiley

'Well fuck me dead!' Sal Mineo says as he puts his arm round my shoulder again and smiles like a young Natalie Wood.

'All that time. And neither of us knew. Christ you poor kid ... stuck out there in bloody Bedford Park. No money, no clothes, reheated casseroles.

'Let's face it, they don't love you. Your Nazi dad thinks you live in a dream world. Your wicked stepmother just thinks you're stupid and impractical. And lazy. Said as much on Wednesday. Treat you like shit. Your brothers have got this time-share deal going with a single brain cell between them. Even your sister's nothing like you. You must've known you were different, special. Now you know why. You're my love-child. You're not a mistake, you're my son and I love you and now I've finally found you nothing will ever ever be the same again, I promise.'

He cups my face gently in his big strong sure brown hands, snares my eyes.

'You don't have to daydream any more. Of course you'll be going to university, and you'll meet lots of new friends there who'll like you just the way you are, and I'll buy you so many books you'll have your own library, and you'll be living here in my house—

Oy!

John's ignoring him.

OY!   *Worm! Didja bringya bathers?*

Nicknames are an artform. A nickname's not the same as an insult or a jokey grammar (John: Johnny: Jon-boy: Johnny-be-good). It's a history a classification a snapshot a prediction a theory a sound-bite. It spreads you out and open like that startled-looking frog in first term Biology.

John's been Worm since late last year by weird and exact consensus. Well it's obvious isn't it? He's thin like he's got tapeworm, he's intestine-thin and coiled like a worm, he's blind-white from being a bookworm safe indoors. Kosta came up with it. Kosta's so completely Kosta he's got no need for nicknames or alibis or homework. Kosta and the others use *Worm* like a steel-tongued hook, paying out the line, teasing it into his gullet, jerking, reeling him back in from wherever he goes in that head of his, back down to us-here-now.

Well   didja?

He (just) stops himself from flinching. They've already forgotten him. His video-eye, his Hitchcock-I shuttles to fit the focus of Neil, the window, the signpost, the seam of shrubs, the serrated horizon, horizon, signpost, shrubs, window, the furred whorl in Neil's left ear.

I'm sitting with him now, down by the oval past the cricket nets after school, under our tree, last of afternoon sun, green-sieved, shadow-mosaic, prickle-clutch of grass under our calves. A few of the others are playing footy half-heartedly too far away to hear or take any notice. We talk, both of us, him actually talking to me as me not me as Dear John. We talk of futures we'll never have. We say university and mean factory or shop or dole. We say friends forever, mean not-phoning

*and busyness and moving interstate. We're sad but
we're together. His ear's spot-lit, back-lit, honey-gold,
too tender to believe.*

*I want to reach across and bite it gently, just above
the lobe. I do. He lets me. He likes it. Neil.
NeilNeilNeil*

He doesn't look like a worm really. He looks like Audrey
Hepburn on stilts with acne. Cadbury almond chocolate
eyes, face of a Burmese cat in the vet's waiting room.
He's almost, very almost, sixteen. Nothing fits right,
nothing looks right. Not that it matters much since no
one looks at him, really looks, except the-woman-Dad-
married and then it's only to comb the hair or straighten
up or take the good school shoes off or whatever. His
body's treacherous and under siege, always nearly about
to blurt out his secrets. He's sure what's twisted in him,
what's wrong with him, will show up somewhere sometime. He thinks he's growing into a tabloid-TV face
pervert   PERVERT fat old man running scared on
spiderlegs, run to ground, sweaty jowls and vein-
splotched, up against his own car, pinned through again
and again with sharp lights and microphones.

The clues are all there. The head-down dash on sports
days from benches to showers, lather cover-up, manoeu-
vres with towel and undies, not looking NOT LOOK-
ING at Neil's, which is wide and stubby and very uncir-
cumcised, like a discarded tennis sock with a hole in the
toe. The porn he's hiding inside his head with him and
Kosta hard at it, they'll see it in the holograms of his
eyes. The loneliness of his legs in these bloody surrender-
flag white sports shorts, shirt tucked too neatly in, fid-
dling with his hair, daydreaming again, running his
thoughts softly over the secrets he's been given as 11C's

father-confessor, the prissy way he's sitting — right here, now, in the bus, he's giving himself away and pretty soon someone'll crack the code, crack him wide wide naked helpless open THERE that's what it is not shy not strange not smart not loner   NO   much much simpler   *faggotpoofqueer* obvious of course well we always thought knew of course knew all along neon-signed all over himself for the whole school world father to see.

For now, though, it's just a distance, difference. Manageable. He's got friends: Neil (sigh), Kathie, Jenny, Mary,   Mike   sort of Fiona (spose) oh, and Cameron. Places to sit down next to in class and safe lunchtime territory. Questions follow-ups topics prepared the night before so talk can stretch easy elastic between classrooms and classes and waiting for teachers to turn up and walking home. He's trust-able, he listens, he's got a solid gravity in lieu of being real or John or someone to do things with. So he hears all about the feral boyfriend and factional brawls and the small claims tribunal of loyalty and hearts smashed by crushes oh and aches and plans and tears and periods   all of it. And he intercedes, fixes, understands, believes. Very good at being shocked and knows exactly how you feel. Gives advice which no one takes but takes it and them seriously. Though his compassion's sneaky, only a few good intentions away from contempt as a kind of revenge. Meanwhile he practises his signature over and over, greedy for growing up.

Kosta and the rest, he lets them tease him enough to make a hobby out of him, spare-time instead of a target. He knows they know he knows they know. But they don't have a word for it yet so it can't be punched, can't be blackmailed or bartered, or strip-searched up against the fence, big scrum and tag-team humiliation like they did to that kid with the birthmark. Or making gauntlets down the corridors, cruel surgical mimics and fun-fair mirrors. Did that with the stu-stu-stu-utt-er-er.

You have to be careful. You have to be prepared. You have to be normal.

No that's wrong. They've got words for it, more words than they know what to do with, names like Chinese burns, insults for throwing and hitting, catching and pelting back, small hard sticks and stones of words that bruise and cut and stun and leave you standing all alone and looked-at, haemorrhaging gentlygently-stoic. But hey it's just words. No one believes in them. *Poofta's* a threat or pay-back or lay-by, or knee-jerk joke or soccer bum-pat irony, or a carnival on TV or an exposé in a paper or a rumour round a nightclub or a sack of bloody deboned pervert in a park, not the kid you're sitting across from.

The shudder-sway of the bus slides him along imperceptibly over, comfortably close to Neil's thigh. Drives him fuckin insane. Neil's cock-dead. Pimples *yes* baby-muscle *yes* suddenly tall *yes* gangly *yes* armpit under-growth *yes* but he's supposed to start getting interested in girls or boys or wanking or SOMETHING. Once, New Year's Eve, this year? yes, this year, they shared a makeshift bed. The house was crammed with relatives, workmates, friends and acquaintances everyone thought someone else had invited and by about two or three o'clock snoring shadows were piling up all over the place, so the kids got shunted out the backyard with sofa cushions and sheets.

All those sticky nights spent dreaming up seduction scenarios complete with dialogue, all that useful instruction from toilet walls at the Marion shops (o yes he's read the hard scrabbling graffiti, he knows what goes on), a whole puberty's worth of frustrated suspense damming up his balls. There'll never be a better chance. He lay there stiff and stiff, sweating high-octane testosterone. Nothing. Not even an accidental goose-bumply brush of skin on skin or skin on flannelette.

> *'But John—*   *What if—'*
> *'They won't be home for ages.   Come on.   Just—*
> *That's it.'*
> *'Maybe we sh—'*
> *I plug his mouth with my tongue.*

Nothing.

John's step-mum wonders how she manages to get through her hand cream so quick. He will have the softest, smoothest, most prematurely unwrinkled penis in history.

He repositions his clipboard over his pop-up toaster cock, strenuously not noticing the satin velcro of Neil's leg on his. This is a real live Geography excursion to Maslins Beach and there's work to do: cross-sections, drawings, rock classification, fossil identification, erosion patterns, pages and pages of stuff. Just as well. Maslins is, as everyone knows, the first and best, the most infamous, the nudest, nude beach. It's an icon and a tourist attraction. Why, it's historic. But after all it's a weekday and it's been done every year in Geography for oh ages and there's the two teachers of course and it's for proper marks. So parents bribed their four-square Adelaide imaginations and dutifully signed the form to let their little darlings loose on sunny expanses of sand, sea and pubic hair.

Bets have been laid. A tit-spotting contest. Someone's managed to smuggle his dad's camera and can't stop grinning inanely at nobody in particular. Anatomy and rumours exploded out of all proportion. Somebody, probably Pete, knowing Pete, started up this thing about Maslins being a gay beach sort of in some bits, getting off in the bushes and all sorts of sick stuff. As if. Where'd he get a dumb idea like that? Probably made the whole thing up. John doesn't believe it for a minute. Can't afford to. He's already under suspicion, under glass, eyes all over him, body as lie-detector, monitoring give-aways. Where's he looking? What's he not looking at?

I've stopped to take a closer look at the layering of rock down near the bottom of the cliff. I do a quick sketch. We were the stragglers, the F Group bringing up the rear. By the time I look up, the others have gone gone?! Yep. The shitheads have left me way behind. So here I am, alone, on a nude, a nude gay beach. Something makes me look up to the left and there's this man, this naked man, this big tanned naked man, this huge bronzed COCK standing right up there grinning at me. He moves his hand down——

No.

So. Focus. He listens as Mr McKenzie explains the assessment again — essay due in a fortnight – all answers to Section A from listening CAREFULLY   Kosta? THANK you listening carefully as he explains things as they go — Section B multiple choice aaaaaand Section C's the one to be done in small groups. Some of the stuff's pretty easy. Should be okay.

The bus smells of sweaty schoolbags and airless excitement, tense with the effort of unconcern. Everybody's talking intently past each other in cramped anticipation. A bunched pack of blonde ponytails up to the right are scavenging the tripe left over from yesterday's gossip. Behind him, the big boys, real boys, men in training, tussling with invisible, conversational ruckrovers or half-fronts or whateverthehell they're called. Someone up the front's just finished a joke and giggles unwind in a long thread down the aisle like goldfish bubbles. Fiona (Fiona Mac not Fiona B) is preening again (still), fixing fringe and mascara smudge and button: cleavage ratio with absent-minded precision, using Mary as a rear-view mirror. Two rows up Mike's drumming out the rhythm of his patience on the back of the seat in front of him.

Testing testing 1 2 3 they're rehearsing themselves, their selves, trying out catch-phrases and me-gestures and expensive hair and other people's voices, always and already betrayed into awkward self-conscious grace. They're all all so careful, so prepared, so normal. 2-D. Pixillated. Syndicated. Broadcast. Like sands through the hourglass so the days of their ordinary lives will dribble past, minor drama by docudrama by melodrama, in simple predictable episodes. Safe in a box in a family room in a box just like all the other boxes in the street. They'll never get out, never know they're in.

He shutter-clicks his eyes closed, wishes he were wishes he could be someone   someone else, somewhere else, anyone anywhere but this, this crappy old re-run of a sci fi movie he's stuck in, like *Invasion of the Bodysnatchers*, like an alien who's snatched the wrong body. Wrong everything. 'Home' flashes up on the screen of his eyelids. Home sweet fucking home.

Semi-detached, brick, brick the colour of spilt curry powder, with a corrugated iron roof that talks at night, a doll's-house porch, consumptive eucalypt out the front, couch-grass out the back. Beige blinds with scalloped edges and grubby tassels, foot-printed lino, something stained and hard that used to be carpet. Through here. Mind the nail. The Boys' Room. Same shape and position and paint-job as next door, with whom they share a wall, fence and every childhood disease known to mothers. Same as the one behind too. Same as all the others. This is Housing Trust. Come out the back. Row on row on row on row and every one the same. Cyclone-wire fences make the neighbourhood into graph-paper. Let's play connect-the-Hills-Hoists.

WELCOME TO BEDFORD PARK, HOME OF THE MITSUBISHI FACTORY into which Dad disappears each day, robot-Dad, detailer on an assembly line sucking up dads from all over the Trust and spitting them out the other end exhausted, empty, needing to be put back together again with a stubbie and something hot and filling and small talk chucked over his shoulder to the kitchen and a bit of peace and bloody quiet so DON'T nag me no I'm busy go ask your Mum and for Christ's sake shutup when the news comes on okay? The kids become furniture till God the Father's been appeased. So weeknights, after dinner while current affairs fill the lounge room, John sits on his bunk (top one, after a tough campaign), gazing out the window, polishing, polishing his dreams. And way up the top of the hill Flinders University squats and shits all over him, laughing down at shabby fantasies and an uninnocent boy.

Goes back with his video-eye to panning out the window at the wheatfields and the cars strobing by as if this were an ordinary day.

Cut to a drop of sweat on the back of Neil's neck. Close-up.   Closer. Crystal ball suspended by a hair. Fade to white.

◄◄ ◄◄ ◄◄ ►► ►► ►►

They spill out of the bus. John bursts from an embolism of uniforms and chatter into a souvenir shop postcard. He runs his zoom-lens Attenborough-I along the ants conga-ing down a crevasse in the carpark bitumen, past a fence of dirty shoes and shins, along the driftwood curve of the cliff's edge, the costume-jewellery blue of the sea and up into the bubble of sky, a different blue, colour of a washing-powder TV commercial. Then of course he feels a bit dizzy, wonders if anyone saw him. Roll-call. Division into groups. The alphabet's conspired against him again. Kosta's in his group.

Mr McKenzie darts round the edges of the mob, growling and yapping at the last few strays, and herds them all down the narrow steps notched deep down the rockface. Miss Blazey the grey-haired mongrel rides shot-gun at the back. In twos and threes and concertina pile-ups they clomp down, round to the right, down again (longer and steeper than it looked from up there) till suddenly beach, fine white sand eddies and sucks at their shoes. Back to work. At excruciating glacial pace Mr McKenzie recites the aeons of geriatric ship-in-bottle patience, the monumental church-fete craftwork, that made these cliffs with their strange neatly arranged esca-lator of colours from off-white to scab-brown. With an effort he reduces all this so it can fit on two pages of thir-ty short-answer questions. In his teacher's mousetrap mouth it turns into Geography and Geology, processes and events, times and names, facts and for fuck's sake is he ever going to shutup?

No. Pauses only to check that brains and biros are keeping up.

Still talking talkingtalking at them, simultaneously translating landscape to diagram, he moves them on in orderly manner to the rockpools, neverending bloody fossil sites, then the reef, then right up near the southern point where tusked rocks chew on the surf and spit it back. By now it's early afternoon. Time's clogged with boredom. The air's groggy and the mob's getting restless. September sun pipes through their bones like a glass-blower, clear and breathy. Into the non-stop flowchart of words Miss Blazey levers a rude irrelevancy

Umm sorry to—but perhaps—it's nearly 1.00 after all and

And he nearly forgot lunch. So he shepherds them back along the beach, leadeth them beside unstill waters and maketh them lie down in bruise-blue shade, eat, drink and do fiddly things with contour maps and cross-sections.

In the movie gospel according to John what's needed here is a helicopter shot, one of those long swoops on smooth tracks of air that take it all in: you could come in from high up above the turret of rock hacked off by the sea and then along—

and hey hey for Chrissake can someone can you know how this works? what're we sposed to

Mike again. You only ever hear bits of what he's saying because he talks as if he's pissing hands-free, back and forth in semicircles. Gives people a chance to ignore him without anyone having to notice he's been ignored. Plus he's got a new haircut so he's extra defensively talky. It's a flat-top. Head up, back straight, all proud perpendicularity. Like a helipad for flies. John helps him out locating co-ordinates on the grid map then, quietly patient and vain, does the same for Neil. Kosta's wincing the muscles in his left forearm   boredboredboredbored bored bored BORED, making symmetrical divots in the sand. John's surreptitiously watching his face for light-bulbs. Kosta's got the face of a Ken doll really lightly roasted on a barbecue and when he has an idea, some brilliant shit-stirring plan, he gets this pitbull grin and frowns all the time like he's thinking vewy vewy hard. Yep, there it is. Shit. Kosta's hangers-on and laughers-with have read the signs too and they gather round, cats to an open fridge door.

Then everyone's up and off again. The Leyland Brothers voiceover starts itself up and loops round them as they walk and scribble in their clipboards. But by now they're irresistibly close to the Unclad Bathing bits. Everyone jockeys for positions that'll let them seem like they're busy taking notes while actually looking, binocular-wide-eyed, at the bodies behind Miss Blazey. There's a woman who sort of looks famous, in huge sunglasses under an even huger hat, wearing a tourniquet bikini and glaring right back at them. Mr McKenzie again issues his pointless blanket ban — No Ogling or Laughing – and they move quickly and quietQUIETLY! thankyou on to the next spot, giving nudity as wide a berth as possible. While, of course, ogling and laughing. There are topless women sitting up reading and womenless men suspiciously sharing a towel. A man shaped like a bean-bag is paddling in the shallows. There are middle-aged (old, inconceivably old) women lying on their stomachs. They have bums like slightly ajar leather handbags. There are women spread out luxurious on their backs, gently frying their breasts sunny-side up. They can't be certain from here but Mary and Fiona are pretty sure they've just seen cellulite in the wild. You'd think *Women's Weekly* would've warned them.

In hissed exchanges the boys tot up their tit totals but it's fast losing its appeal. Bit of a fizzer really. No-one seems to be embarrassed or guilty or sexy or on the prowl. They're all just sitting round like they've got their everyday clothes on. The Emperor's old clothes. BorrrrrrrrrrRING. Something'll have to be done about this.

Kosta's hand shoots up Heil Hitler *Scuse me! Sorry! Sir? Mr McKenzie?* John thinks *Here it comes.* The geology tape (Side B) in Mr McKenzie's mouth clicks off. He glares at the kid, as close to hatred as teachers are trained not to get.

What is it? on a leash, pulled back to classroom acoustics.

I know I went before but I really desperately proud of that one *desperately need to go to the toilet again. Sir.* And against the hard silence throws *Sorry Sir.*

And you can't wait till we get down that end of the beach?

Ummmmmm   I don't think so and smiles a hapless not-my-fault shrug.

I suppose, if you gotta go it's a weak attempt at schoolboy humour, he knows, but he's calculating whether he can spare Miss Blazey and clearly can't *then you gotta go* so he looks round the avid faces all dying to see what Kosta's got planned. *But* still looking round, this time for someone, a victim *but John yes you John can go with you.* A kidney-punch pause and John realises at the same time what Mr McKenzie means and that he's been made a police escort—and accomplice—and scapegoat. Because Kosta's gonna pull Christ knows what stunt for which, as deputy sheriff, John can neatly take the blame. Shit. *Just to make sure you don't get lost.* Everyone goes tensely silent, as all good circus audiences do when waiting for someone to fall off, be eaten, get stabbed. *Back here in fifteen minutes got it?*

Kosta's hamming it up for all his fans. Cocks his head to one side, skewers John with his complicated eyes, crow at worm. And Worm he is again again. He scrambles to catch up with Kosta, who's grinding pelvic gears just in case the 36D-cup blonde down by the surfline can see him from there, and she obviously can't so he turns his best spotlight grin on John and wonders if maybe he'd like to come in and hold it for him? It's top quality meat. Still no?

Well you can wait out here then okay?

So here he is, playing sentry, being careful, prepared—prepared for anything. Acts normal, walks round to the side to check for leaking cigarette smoke. Nothing. Back again to wait. And wait. Waits for ten minutes before going in. Empty of course. Fuckin hell. Probably just snuck off somewhere safe for a smoke or joint or what-ever. So he checks round the back, down by the bushes —he won't have risked the kiosk or the other carpark — then along the scrub at the foot of the hills, beginning now to panic since there doesn't seem to be much cover anywhere else and the rest of the class is getting slowly closer and Mr McKenzie's looking this way but where the fuck else could he be? Then gets to the mudcliffs and finds a gully cut deep into the base but not deep enough to hide in, then another, this one going a few metres back — but no, no one there. And another, steep-walled like a winding alleyway and he darts down it and as he goes it widens to a cul-de-sac nothing, some-one's hat but that's it. Out again and to the next one, same as the last but with sloping, climbable sides so he's doing a sort of bifocal flip from the ground then up the scrubby slope, and he's thinking *this is stupid, the shithead could be just about*

suddenly two men   a lifeguard-brown back clutching hands flurry of towels   T-shirt   covering straightening up and   adjusting.

They stare back at him and try, but not too hard, to look sheepish. The one with the crewcut smiles into a cough then, startled, looks past John.

FAAAAAAAAAAAAAAAAAAAAAAAAAGGOTS!

John spins and freezes like a still shot from a bad old black and white thriller.

Kosta. Behind Kosta, his sidekicks, then everyone.

Wo! Hey guys! Found some faaaaaaggots! The voice tightens round John.

Timing's everything. Kosta holds up something small and wobbly EXHIBIT A to show the gathering crowd, walks it up and down for all to examine, courtroom solemn since they're gathered on the edge of an accusation or arrest. It's a sad little wrinkled balloon. It's a knotted used condom. A hiccup of giggly shock goes up.

It's not mine! John could've nearly says *I wasn't I didn't* but denying anything means admitting something so he shuts up.

Slowly, deliberately folds his arms, raises an eyebrow, shakes his head, master at naughty dog. It convinces no one.

His heart's beating him to death.

Scrabbling behind his back. Can't even turn round. The two men disappear out of the corner of his eye, heading for kiosk and anonymity. And he's alone. No he's not. In among the bullring stares he finds a real face. Neil. But Neil's looking at the condom, Kosta, the ground, back for Mr McKenzie, Kosta, the condom. Won't meet anyone's eyes though he must *he must* feel

John's petitioning him. In extreme close-up on his neck below his left ear a pulse hammers hammers out *careful prepared normal* careful now be careful. And Neil does nothing, says nothing, steps back into the laughing amoeba of faces. Down the other end Mr McKenzie gets extruded, red-blotched and out of breath.

I don't know what's happened here and I don't want to alright? Quiet please. Thankyou. No I don't care — NO — don't bother with the explanations just — quiET! THANKyou. Listen up. We're running out of time. Kosta, I'll deal with you when we get back. Put that bloody thing in the bin. NOW! Up there near the toilets and make sure you wash your hands.

And be careful. Hurry UP! John, get back over here with the others. We're dividing into groups for Section C. Now! Don't wander, don't dawdle. You all know your group. No. 1 here, No. 2 there, No. 3 just there, No. 4 over there, No. 5 you'll be with me, No. 6 with Miss Blazey come on come ON hurry it up! You'll all have read the instructions on the way here like I told you to so you know what to do now do it.

The rest of the afternoon never happens. It's not him, can't have happened, isn't real, can't be happening so it's a blank. No — there's a moment, a single frame, he'll take home and hide for later. A kid whose name he can't remember, in the group thing, whatever they were doing, looking for something in the scrub and Kosta's got his hooks in, fag-baiting for spectator sport, sly and hilarious and alimentary and unstoppably inventive and on and on and and this kid saw, and knew, and smiled. At John. Cheeks flambéd in acne and brave shyness but the smile's clear and given.

Neil-less, flayed way past naked, it's all he has.

⏮ ◀◀ ◀◀ ▶▶ ▶▶ ⏭

Back in the bus his eyes are shut. He's sitting seven seats away from Neil, next to someone he doesn't know. His video-I's turned off. His face is locked, untenanted. He's more careful now. And prepared. In-different, since not normal.

'And this,' James Dean says with that slow-fuse smile, 'this is the room you'll be sharing with Neil. Welcome home.'

About the Contributors

Robert Dessaix is a well-known ABC broadcaster, essayist and literary commentator. He is the editor of *Australian Gay and Lesbian Writing: an Anthology* (Oxford University Press) and his most recent book is the autobiographical *A Mother's Disgrace* (Angus & Robertson, 1994).

Kerry Greenwood has worked as a folk singer, a factory hand, a producer, a translator, a costume maker and a cook and currently works part time for the Legal Aid Commission as an advocate in Magistrates' Courts. She has written several plays, eight novels about 1920s sleuth Phryne Fisher, two historical novels, *The Childstone Cycle* and *Cassandra*, and a history of the Springvale Legal Service, as well as editing *The Thing She Loves*, a book of essays on female murderers, and co-writing *Recipes for Crime* with Jenny Pausacker. She lives with a registered Wizard.

Kerry comments: 'I saw Jean Moulin's memorial, a naked marble man with a sword across his knees, in the Jardin Communal in Béziers. I was so impressed that I inquired further and found that he was the Resistance hero Max. It has been suggested that Jean himself was gay. It was a pretty day in the garden and there were ducks and irises and this story suggested itself.'

Carol Jones is the doting mother of two young children and the doting editor of three children's magazines — and she certainly knows which job is the more difficult. Born in Brisbane in 1957, she has lived in Melbourne since childhood, apart from a brief interlude teaching in Victoria's Western District. She has worked as a teacher for ten years and as a children's magazine editor for seven years and she is currently editing the magazines *Pursuit* and *Comet*. Her first novel for young adults, *Real Girls*, was followed by a companion novel, *Sibs*, and she is also the author of *Going De Loco*, a wacky mystery for eight to twelve year olds.

Dean Kiley is a young writer and Australian Literature Honours student who lives in, but is not, North Shore Sydney. When he's not queer, he's queering; he's a devout collector of bad habits and good friends; he will make a great academic and wife some day. He is nomadic, writes to and for people rather than places or markets and feels claustrophobic in pigeonholes. He has won first and third prizes respectively for the 1993 and 1995 national OutRage Short Story Competition and has been published in *Australian Book Review*, *OutRage*, *Island*, *Republica*, *BURN*, *Siglo*, *Southern Review*, *Spindrift*, *Antithesis*, *Fruit* and the 1993 and 1995 *OutRage* Short Story anthologies. His first book, *and that's final*, was published by BlackWattle Press in August 1995.

Nigel Krauth's publications include *Matilda, My Darling, The Bathing-Machine Called the Twentieth Century, JF Was Here* and three novels for teenagers co-written with

Caron Krauth. Nigel grew up in Sydney and Newcastle and now lives on Tamborine Mountain, near the Gold Coast. His writing has won national awards. He understands that reality and fiction are the same thing – a riddle with a painful answer.

John Lonie's short stories are in all major Australian gay anthologies, as well as in collections in the United States and Europe. His major occupation, however, is as a screenwriter. Among his credits are the mini-series *True Believers* and *The Paper Man*. A Queenslander, he lives at Bondi and has just completed a screenplay for producer Sue Milliken.

Caroline Macdonald has lived in Australia since 1984, the year after her first novel *Elephant Rock* was published. Since then she has continued to write for younger readers — novels including *The Lake at the End of the World*, *Speaking to Miranda*, *Secret Lives* and *Spider Mansion*. She has been writing full time since 1988 and lives in Adelaide.

Ian MacNeill's novel for adolescents, *Red and Silver*, was published in 1992. Other work includes *Beaches and Billabongs* (a novel), *TV Tricks* (poetry) and a collection of gay writings, *Libbing*. His play *Hors de Combat* was performed as part of the 1992 Mardi Gras festival and his stories, articles and criticism have appeared in the gay and lesbian press over many years.

Merrilee Moss is a playwright and novelist who lectures in writing at Victoria University. Her plays, which have toured theatres and community venues all over Australia, include *If Looks Could Kill*, *Over the Hill*,

Empty Suitcases and *Sez Who?!* Moss began writing for young people in 1987 when she was inspired to contribute to the Dolly Fiction romance series. (Her titles include *Stroke of Luck*, *Behind the Scenes* and *Forget Me Not*.) In collaboration with Jenny Pausacker, Moss has also written the eight book adventure/romance series *Hot Pursuit* (Penguin). Her latest novel, *Thriller and Me*, was published by Silver Gum Press in 1994.

Bron Nicholls has worked at many jobs to support her writing habit; they include nursing, signwriting, sorting apricots in a canning factory, teaching, illustrating and theatre set painting. Her published novels are *Three Way Street* (shortlisted for the 1983 Children's Book of the Year award), *Mullaway* for young adults (made into a feature film) and *Reasons of the Heart* for adults. Bron has also written TV scripts for a school science show and many plays for youth theatre. Her first published book was a drama text, *Move!*, and her first-ever novel, written at age twelve, was about the small country town of her childhood.

Helen Pausacker was born in 1954 in Melbourne and has been involved with lesbian and gay male coalition groups since 1979, although recently she has been taking long service leave from activism. She has worked part time in a range of jobs, among them kitchen hand, secretary, administrative assistant, library assistant, research assistant and teacher. Her short stories have been published in a variety of anthologies and magazines, including *Falling for Grace* (BlackWattle, 1993), *OutRage 1995 Gay and Lesbian Short Story Anthology* (Bluestone) and *Death of a Mother* (Harper Collins, 1994).

Jenny Pausacker was born in 1948. She has written eleven books for children and young adults and twenty-seven romances and thrillers for teenagers or adults (under a variety of pseudonyms), as well as co-editing *Moments of Desire* with Susan Hawthorne. Her young adult novel *What Are Ya?*, winner of the 1985 Angus and Robertson Junior Writers Fellowship, was the first Australian children's book with a gay main character and her short stories about young lesbians and gay men have appeared in the anthologies *Landmarks*, *Families*, *Australian Gay and Lesbian Writing*, *The Phone Book* and *Ready or Not*. *Mr Enigmatic*, The sequel to *What Are Ya?* won the 1995 Ethel Turner Prize for children's literature in The N.S.W. Premier's Awards.

Dorothy Porter. Born 1954. Has published six books of poetry, including *Driving Too Fast* (UQP 1989) and the verse novel *Akhenaten* (UQP 1992). The most recent, *The Monkey's Mask* (Hyland House 1994), a detective thriller verse novel, won the Age Book of the Year for Poetry in 1994, was joint winner of the National Book Council Award for Poetry in 1995 and has been published in the USA. It is currently in its third printing and the film rights have been sold. Dorothy's seventh collection of poetry is *Crete* (Hyland House 1996) and she has also published two novels for teenagers. *Rookwood* (UQP 1991) and *The Witch Number* (UQP 1993). She is currently living in Melbourne.

Cameron Sharp now lives in Wollongong with a vegie patch and a bandicoot colony. He writes, reads, signs, swims and still protests with gusto. Given two weeks free from all other commitments, he would spend it wilderness walking. He is thirty-four.

Lucy Sussex was born in New Zealand in 1957 and works as a researcher, freelance author and editor. She has published widely, writing anything from reviews and literary criticism to horror and detective stories. She is also a literary archaeologist, rediscovering and republishing the nineteenth-century Australian crime writers Mary Fortune and Ellen Davitt. Her short story 'My Lady Tongue' won a Ditmar (Australian Science Fiction Achievement Award) in 1988. In 1994 she was a judge for the international Tiptree award which honours speculative fiction exploring notions of gender. She has edited four anthologies, three science fiction and one crime.

Sarah Walker was born in 1965. She has a BA in Communications and is a Sydney-based writer and journalist. Her first novel for teenagers will be published by Pan Macmillan in 1996. She has taught writing at the University of Western Sydney and is currently Chief Sub-Editor at *News Weekly* magazine.

Nadia Wheatley began writing fiction in 1976, after completing postgraduate work in Australian history. Her first book, *Five Times Dizzy*, received the New South Wales Premier's Special Children's Book Award in 1983 and was produced as a twelve part television series. Her other work for children includes *My Place* (Australian Children's Book Council Book of the Year for Younger Readers in 1988) and *Lucy in the Leap Year* (an Honour Book in the 1994 Children's Book Council Awards). In the young adult field Nadia Wheatley has written the novels *The House that was Eureka* (winner of the New South Wales Premier's Children's Book Award in 1986) and *The Blooding*. Her first collection of short stories, *The Night Tolkien Died*, was an Honour Book in the

Older Readers section of the 1995 Children's Book Council Awards.

Ben Widdicombe was born in 1970. He writes on gay and lesbian issues for newspapers and magazines in the UK, USA and Australia and his fiction has been published in Australia and Canada. He is currently working as a journalist for the Sydney *Star Observer*. He had a long row with the editor of this anthology over the use of the word 'gotten', which he lost.